THE NEXT WORLD

GERRY GRIFFITHS

SEVERED PRESS
HOBART TASMANIA

THE NEXT WORLD

DEDICATION

For the boys,
Harry and Frankie

1

Chimola sat alone while the others huddled around the campfire at the base of the dry riverbed. He could hear their whispering voices under the crackling of the burning wood. The steep walls of the gully were high enough so that the fire could not be seen from afar.

Even though they were miles from the national park, there was always the threat of discovery by heavily armed park rangers out on extended nighttime patrols.

A poacher laughed and the others joined in. Chimola knew they were mocking him though he doubted if Duna, their boss man, saw any humor in what had happened during their latest kill. After they had downed the rhino, it had been Chimola's job with the chainsaw. Into the first cut, Chimola had angled the rotating blade wrong and the link had snapped on the chain, rendering the critical equipment useless.

Duna had been furious, as they were forced to resort to their axes and machetes, strenuous and messy work in the blistering African heat.

Even though Chimola sat fifty feet away from the truck, he could smell the rotting flesh still attached to the rendered horn under the tarp on the flatbed.

Chimola picked up his plastic bottle of *waregi*, the Ugandans' word for "war gin," and chugged another swig of the rotgut moonshine. By the sound of the other poachers, they too were sharing the village-made hooch and would soon be passed out.

Chimola leaned back on his blanket and gazed up at the immense nightscape of stars. A green streak shot across the sky. For the past few nights, he had seen more of the green flashes darting past the stars and disappearing into the horizon.

He reached over and took another gulp of the waregi.

His eyelids began to droop as the quick-acting alcohol pulled him into a body-numbing slumber.

Chimola had been sound asleep for two hours when the giant tsetse fly alighted on his bare chest and folded its wings on its back. The fly's head and thorax together were as big as a football. As soon as the insect bit into Chimola's neck, microscopic trypanosome parasites immediately entered his bloodstream—like newborn tadpoles discovering the wonders of a pond—and the sleeping sickness carriers swam freely throughout the man's body.

The enormous fly raised its two front legs, fitfully cleaned its proboscis, and flew off into the night.

At daybreak, the poachers packed up the truck.

Duna ordered one of his men to roust Chimola, but no matter how hard the man tried, Chimola would not wake up.

Still angry and not wanting to waste any more time, Duna decided to leave Chimola behind, and they all got in the truck and drove off.

Chimola continued to sleep through most of the morning, even when three male lions wandered down into the coulee. The big cats paced around Chimola's still body then moved in and lay on their bellies to feed on the sleeping man.

It was early afternoon when the lions left, and the patiently awaiting vultures in a nearby tree descended to pick at the carcass.

By nightfall, a clan of hyenas found Chimola's skeletal remains and chewed up his bones.

Come morning, Chimola was nothing more than wind-blown dust on the savanna.

2

Frank Travis peered out his portal window and watched the wildebeest as the plane passed over the stampeding herd. He pressed his cheek against the glass and could see the tiny structures of the Tomie Private Wildlife Reserve and the dirt airstrip, just a few miles ahead.

"We're just about there," Frank said as he turned to his wife, Wanda, seated across the narrow aisle of the ten-passenger Beechcraft.

Wanda glanced over. "I can't believe you talked me into this."

"Can you think of a better place to spend our anniversary?"

"Uh, yeah. Plenty."

"Trust me, you're going to love it."

"I've heard that one before."

"Hey, this is a great opportunity for Ally," Frank said. "I wrote Dr. Tomie and she is more than glad to take Ally under her wing."

"Thank God, Ally got her athletic scholarship. UC Davis isn't cheap."

"No, but they do have one of the best veterinarian programs in the country. That and I now have a ride-along in the commuter lane."

"Any idea when they might offer you the position?"

"Head of the Entomology Department? Soon, I hope. Can't wait to move into that corner office."

"Don't you mean stodgy bottom-floor cubical?"

"Well, it does have a window." Frank glanced out and saw they were descending. "Looks like we're getting ready to land."

Wanda glanced over her shoulder at the seat behind Frank. "How are you doing, Dilly?"

Eight-year-old Dillon Rafferty looked up from his DC Comic. "What?"

Wanda had to raise her voice so she could be heard over the thrum of the twin turboprops outside. "We're just about there, honey."

"Can we eat?" the boy shouted back.

"Soon," Wanda promised. She leaned over the armrest and looked back at her teenage daughter, Ally, sitting two seats back, and gave her a little wave.

Ally smiled and reached across the aisle, nudging her twenty-one-year-old brother, Ryan.

They both leaned out and looked at their mother.

"Looks like we're about to touch down," Wanda told them and they both nodded.

In less than ten minutes they were on the ground. The uniformed pilot exited the cockpit and smiled as he squeezed down the aisle to the rear of the plane. He opened the hatch door and lowered the stairs. "Hope you enjoyed your flight. See you all in a week," he said as Frank and his family grabbed their luggage and disembarked the plane one at a time.

Once everyone was off the plane, a large safari Jeep with three rows of passenger seats rolled up. An African man wearing a tan shirt and cargo shorts stepped out from behind the steering wheel to greet them.

"Hello. I am Isoba."

Frank walked up and shook the man's hand. "I'm Frank Travis and this is my family." Frank took a moment to introduce everyone and they graciously exchanged handshakes.

An African woman wearing similar attire as the driver climbed out of the safari Jeep from the front passenger seat.

Isoba turned and said, "This is my oldest daughter, Adanna."

"Pleased to meet you," Adanna said. She took a moment to shake everyone's hand.

"So, what it is you do here?" Wanda asked when she noticed that Isoba and his daughter were both wearing sidearms.

"Our job is to protect the reserve," Isoba said.

"And to ensure your safety," Adanna added. "That way we hope you will enjoy your stay with us."

"My wife, Wanda, is also in law enforcement," Frank said proudly.

"Is that so?" Isoba said with great interest.

"I'm just a sheriff in a sleepy town; nothing special."

Isoba nodded and then gestured toward the Jeep. "Come. We will show you to your cottages."

3

"This is nice," Wanda said as she stepped inside the cottage. The circular room had an overhead fan mounted on a beam stretched under the high-domed ceiling and decorative sconce lighting on the plastered beige walls. A crème-colored settee faced a recessed fireplace. A bedspread with a zebra pattern covered the queen-size bed.

There was a sitting area with two armchairs facing a sliding glass door that looked out on a patio and, beyond, the sprawling savanna that stretched for miles.

Frank came in and put their travel bags next to a small dresser positioned under a large framed photograph of antelopes leaping across the grassland.

"What did you call this little adventure of ours again?" Wanda asked.

"A working vacation," Frank replied, sitting on the edge of the bed. "Originally, I was going to book one of those fancy safari packages. That was until Dr. Tomie came to the campus and gave a powerful speech about wildlife conservation and how more people should get involved in protecting the planet."

"Well, I'm all for that."

"Besides, I know how you hate just sitting around, doing nothing."

"Oh, you mean like on a beach, sipping a strawberry daiquiri on some Hawaiian island."

"Definitely not your style." Frank got up and unzipped one of their bags, but Wanda's hand on his arm stopped him.

"How about we unpack later. I'd like to go meet the doctor."

"Let's go."

Frank and Wanda walked out, turned left, and followed the stone steps that led down a pathway in front of four other similarly designed cottages. Each had a tiled roof with a white railing porch and a window on each side of the front door.

They stopped at the second cottage. The door was open.

"Hey, you guys," Wanda called out. "We're going over to the animal hospital."

Ryan and Dillon stepped out onto the porch.

"I'm hungry," Dillon said.

"Here, eat this." Ryan handed his little brother a packet of peanuts.

Dillon eyed the small bag like it was a plateful of vegetables.

"Come on, we'll grab some food in a bit," Wanda said, not giving Dillon a chance to protest.

Ally was already waiting outside the next cottage.

"Where are we going?" Ally asked.

"Time for the grand tour," Frank said.

They headed to a larger building and saw Isoba standing by the entrance.

"Hello. Do you like your rooms?"

"Oh, yes, thank you," Wanda said.

"Come inside." Isoba opened and held the door for everyone as they stepped through.

A tan woman wearing a denim shirt and jeans was there to greet them. "Welcome. Frank, I'm so glad you and your family could come."

"Dr. Tomie, nice to see you again. Let me introduce my wife, Wanda."

"How do you do, Doctor."

"Please, call me Gayle."

"Okay," Wanda said with a smile. She turned to her children. "This is my oldest son, Ryan; my daughter, Ally; and my boy, Dillon."

"So happy to meet you all," Dr. Tomie said. She looked at Ally. "Your father tells me you're studying to become a veterinarian."

"That's right."

"I was just on my way to surgery. How would you like to assist me?"

"Sure!" Ally replied excitedly.

Dr. Tomie looked at Frank. "You're all welcome to watch."

"Should I stay out here with Dillon?" Wanda asked, thinking the surgery might be too graphic for an eight year old.

"No, no. He'll be fine," Dr. Tomie said with a grin. "We're only pulling a tooth."

Dr. Tomie led the way down a short corridor and opened a door into a large room with an examining table and a sink in a countertop. Cabinets with glass doors and shelves stocked with medical supplies were mounted on one wall.

There were cages of different sizes staggered about the room, some with injured birds like the vulture with the bandaged foot and the parrots with the splints on their wings. A baby antelope was curled up on a blanket. Two wide-eyed lemurs sat at the back of a cage, each missing a limb. A litter of wild dog pups wrestled, spilling water out of their dish.

An African woman stepped into the room. She wore jeans and a scrub top with different types of birds. "Hi, I'm Dayo."

Everyone gave her a friendly smile.

"Dayo is a big help to me in the clinic and will one day make a wonderful doctor," Dr. Tomie said. "And she is Isoba's daughter."

"Oh, so Adanna is your sister," Wanda said.

"Yes, but I am the fun one," Dayo replied. "Adanna is always too serious."

"Dayo, show Ally where she can wash up. She will be assisting us with Sasha."

"This way," Dayo said, and Ally followed.

"You don't mean *the* Sasha?" Frank asked.

"Yes, the very one," Dr. Tomie said proudly.

"Who's Sasha?" Wanda asked.

"Come and see." Dr. Tomie walked into the adjacent room and stood at a glass partition that faced an operating room.

Wanda gasped, "Oh my God!" when she saw the white-coat lioness lying on the operating table. "That's Sasha? She's enormous. How much does she weigh?"

"Well, we just weighed her so we knew how much anesthesia to give her. Would you believe five hundred twenty-three pounds?"

Ally and Dayo entered the operating room through a side door. Ally was wearing a scrub top with tiny elephants. She looked through the observation glass and smiled as if to say *Can you believe I'm really doing this?*

Dayo went over to a cart next to the operating table. She beckoned Ally over and began showing the teenage girl the surgical instruments laid out on a tray. Ally was only a foot away from the big cat's head. Sasha's large fangs protruded out from under her curled upper lip.

Wanda looked at Frank with concern.

"She'll be fine. Sasha's heavily sedated," he assured his wife.

"I had no idea female lions got that big," Wanda said.

"Sasha's quite the celebrity," Dr. Tomie said. "She just made the last issue of *National Geographic*. White lions are quite a rarity. Not to mention one as big as Sasha."

"She's pretty remarkable," Wanda said.

"That she is," Dr. Tomie agreed. "Sasha's one of a kind."

4

Billionaire Tyrone Vane sat in his thousand-dollar-a-day hotel suite and stared at his latest acquisition on the king-size bed.

Made of Damascus steel, it was a thing of beauty meant exclusively for royalty—not a crook that made his fortune ripping off naive first-time homebuyers by conning them into low-interest mortgages on over-valued houses. Every time the foreclosure crisis flooded the market, Vane swooped in and bought up every property he could get his hands on and flipped them for the next wave of gullible families wanting to live the American dream of owning their very own home.

And now he had more money than he knew what to do with.

Which was why he had no qualms buying the most expensive hunting gun in the world—the VO Falcon rifle.

So what if it cost him $820,000; that was nothing to him.

He poured another flute of champagne from the $3,500 bottle of Krug Clos d'Ambonnay and toasted the empty room. He took a sip, glanced over, and saw his reflection in a full-length mirror on the opposite wall. His thick, black hair was slicked back into a ponytail, his gray beard trimmed close to the jaw line. He thought he looked a little paunchy the way he was sitting and sat up straight.

Still admiring himself in the mirror, Vane reached inside the top pocket of his tan safari jacket and took out a thin box of cheroots. He plucked a slim cigar from the box and lit the tip with a gold-plated butane lighter. Taking a drag, he blew out a steady stream of smoke toward the ceiling.

A knock sounded on the hotel door.

Vane got up and strode across the elegant room. He opened the door and waved to the waiter standing in the hall to come in. The man pushed a white linen cart with metal serving dishes into the room and strolled up to a small dining table.

While the waiter set the table and arranged the food dishes, Vane sat back in his chair and looked at pictures from his hunts on his electronic tablet.

The exorbitant lunch consisted of a ten-ounce Wagyu ribeye steak, a miniature tin of Almas Iranian caviar and, for dessert, a Golden Opulence Sundae in a Harcourt crystal goblet and an 18-karat gold spoon with which to eat it.

Once he was done, the server stepped back to await the rich man's approval.

Vane kept flipping through pictures and saying, "Oh my... Now there's a beauty...Will you look at that." Vane glanced up and saw the man waiting. He got up from his chair and walked over to the waiter to show the man the screen.

The waiter politely watched as Vane scrolled from one snapshot to the next.

There was Vane, holding his rifle, standing next to a dead elephant.

Vane kneeling beside a dead moose.

Vane showing off the dead tiger he had killed.

Vane gloating next to a dead grizzly bear.

Vane grinning with one foot on the back leg of a dead rhinoceros.

Vane and a...

"Sir, I really must get back to the kitchen," the waiter said, averting his eyes from the morbid images flicking across the screen.

Vane looked at the man and scowled. "Then I suggest you get going."

The waiter turned, knowing he'd just been stiffed for a tip, and wheeled the cart across the room. He opened the door and disappeared into the hall.

The door closed slowly.

Vane tossed the tablet on the bed, which landed next to an open suitcase.

He leaned down and took out the *National Geographic* magazine that he had recently purchased. An enormous white lioness was on the cover with the caption: Sasha—Super Cat of the Savanna.

As Vane studied the picture he gazed into those amber eyes, imagining he was staring at them down the front sight of his VO Falcon rifle.

5

All precautions had been made to ensure Sasha's procedure went off without a hitch. She was hooked up to an IV of saline and a plastic tube was inserted just inside her gaping mouth so that oxygen could be pumped into her lungs.

Dr. Tomie wore a headlamp on her head so she that she had plenty of light to see inside of the big cat's mouth. She glanced over at Ally. "We were hoping we could salvage the tooth, maybe perform a root canal, but there's too much decay."

"How did you know she was in pain?" Ally asked.

"She's been pawing her mouth. It's very important that lions have good teeth."

"Tell her the story," Dayo said as she injected a long syringe needle into Sasha's gum tissue below the rotted tooth.

"Well, over a hundred years ago workers building a bridge for the Kenya-Uganda Railway were being killed by two lions known as the Tsavo Man-Eaters. They even made a movie about it with Michael Douglas, *The Ghost and the Darkness*," Dr. Tomie said, concentrating on her work as she placed the tip of a chisel at the base of the decayed tooth then slammed the end of the tool with a hammer. She quickly grabbed the uprooted tooth out of the lion's mouth and dropped it in a small tray on the cart.

"In about a nine-month period," she continued, "the lions had killed twenty-eight workers. Some were even ripped from their tents while they slept."

"Oh my gosh," Ally said.

Dayo held a thick gauze compression pad on the bleeding gum.

"Ally, can you take over for Dayo so she can stitch up Sasha?"

"Yes, sure." Ally moved around Dayo and applied pressure to the wound and swabbed away the blood.

Dayo threaded the catgut in the eye of the curved needle.

Dr. Tomie went on with her story as she observed Dayo stitching the lion's gum. "Finally, the engineer of the project had to hire a hunter. When the lions were finally killed, it was later discovered that one of them was suffering from a toothache, which might have attributed to its bad disposition."

"That really happened?" Ally asked as she watched Dayo skillfully sew the hole closed.

"Honest truth," Dr. Tomie said. "It can be very dangerous out here."

"And very beautiful," Dayo said, completing the last stitch and snipping off the end of the catgut.

Ally glanced at the observation window and was happy to see her mother, Frank, Ryan, and Dillon all giving her the thumbs-up.

6

While Ally stayed behind to spend more time with Dr. Tomie and Dayo, Frank and the others continued on through to the rear of the building where an African man wearing a long white shirt, loose trousers, and sandals was waiting by the doorway that led outside.

"This is Gatura, one of many volunteers from a nearby village that come and help take care of the animals," Isoba said.

Gatura gave everyone a big smile.

"I will leave you with Gatura as I and Adanna must go on patrol."

"Then we'll see you later?" Frank asked.

"Perhaps for supper," Isoba replied and walked hastily back down the corridor.

"Come," Gatura said. He stepped out onto the dirt where there were numerous stable-like enclosures, a few small corrals, and a mud-walled building with six steel bar doors. The compound was somewhere around eighty feet by two hundred feet and was further surrounded by a twelve-foot tall cyclone fence.

When Dillon came outside, two white goats with black heads came up to greet him. One of the animals went for the packet of peanuts in the boy's hand.

"Hey, little fella. You want some?" Dillon tore open the bag and shook some peanuts into the palm of his hand. Both goats nibbled at the nuts and slobbered his hand.

"Looks like you found yourself some friends," Frank said.

"Can they come sleep with me?" Dillon asked.

"Maybe another time," Wanda told her son.

Ryan walked over and approached a large dog sitting by a gate.

"I don't recognize this breed," Ryan said.

"Samson is an Anatolian shepherd," Gatura said.

Samson had black ears and a thick, wiry, creamy-white coat. The canine had a similar body type as a yellow Labrador but with a slimmer stomach. He was a whopping 140 pounds.

A rugged four-door truck with big all-terrain tires pulled up outside the gate and stopped. Isoba was behind the wheel. He gave a loud whistle.

Gatura opened the gate and Samson charged out.

Adanna was sitting up front in the passenger seat. She reached back and pushed opened the rear door and Samson jumped in. The door closed when Isoba sped off.

After shutting the gate, Gatura said, "Please, have a look around."

Ryan went over to where an ostrich was standing inside a railed fence. Its right eye was a glazed milky white and looked infected.

He saw a Thompson gazelle with a large boil on its neck that needed to be removed in the next stall.

Dillon ran ahead of Frank and Wanda.

"Slow down," Wanda called out as they passed more animals that were in dire need of medical attention.

Dillon raced around the corner post of a corral. Seconds later, he returned with a three-legged animal walking at his side. "Look what I found."

Wanda took one look at the animal and turned to Frank. "Is that a hyena?"

"Looks like it," Frank replied.

Wanda turned and shouted, "Dillon, get over here now!"

"But Mom..."

"It is all right," Gatura said. "Hobbie is friendly."

To show Wanda there was no danger, Gatura went up to the young hyena and gave him a scratch behind the ear.

"Aren't they supposed to be dangerous?" Wanda asked.

"When we care for them, they learn we mean them no harm. They are grateful. Hobbie was only a pup when Isoba found him. The leg was badly broken and Dr. Tomie could not save it. Hobbie has been here ever since."

"So all the animals are friendly?" Dillon asked.

"No," Gatura said. "The animals out there know only one thing, and that is to stay alive. If they feel threatened, they will not be friendly. So you must be careful."

"So you live near here?" Wanda asked.

"Yes, in my village."

"And others from your village come here to volunteer?" Frank asked.

"Yes. We all do. Dr. Tomie has taught us to care for the animals."

"How big is this reserve?" Wanda asked Gatura, but when he shrugged his shoulders, she looked to Frank for the answer.

"Somewhere over two hundred square miles. I believe there is a national park bordering on two sides of the reserve, the rest being open land."

"Open to poachers," Gatura said with disdain.

"You mean poachers actually come onto the reserve?" Wanda asked.

"Yes. It is Isola and Adanna's job to keep them away."

"Two people to guard two hundred square miles," Wanda said. "That hardly sounds right. Talk about an impossible task."

"Yes," Gatura said. "It is impossible."

7

It took six of the strongest volunteers to carry Sasha to her enclosure and lay her on the straw covered dirt floor to recover from the anesthesia. Dr. Tomie thanked them as they filed out and returned to their duties caring for the other animals.

Ally and Dayo stood at the opened doorway while Dr. Tomie sat beside the big cat and placed the disc-shaped resonator of her stethoscope on Sasha's chest.

"How is she?" Dayo asked.

"Her heart sounds strong," Dr. Tomie replied.

"How old is Sasha?" Ally asked.

"She is almost ten. Lions can live to eighteen years if they remain healthy."

Ally saw Sasha's tail swish in the air. "I think she's waking up."

Sasha slowly opened her eyes.

Dr. Tomie remained beside Sasha and gently stroked the white lioness.

"Shouldn't we be leaving?" Ally asked, stepping back.

"You need not be afraid," Dayo said.

Sasha shifted her body to get her legs under her body and struggled onto her feet. She stood wobbly and almost fell when she took a step but managed to remain standing.

Dr. Tomie stood and walked toward the doorway.

Sasha followed the veterinarian and they came outside.

"She's so tame," Ally said, seeing how docile the huge lioness seemed standing next to the woman a fourth her weight.

"Sasha has learned to trust humans. Which, I'm afraid, makes her very vulnerable, especially to poachers and big game hunters."

"Then why not keep her here?"

"Sasha is an important member of her pride. And she has a cub."

"Is it white like Sasha?" Ally asked.

"Yes, and we have the cub here," Dr. Tomie explained. "The mortality rate of lion cubs is very high: only one out of eight generally survive. That is why we could not separate Sasha from her cub."

"But won't the other lions protect it?"

"Male lions are known to kill the cubs."

"But why would they kill their own kind?" Ally asked in disbelief.

"Animals are not that much different from us. They're merely eliminating the competition should they grow to be stronger. It's rather common for one species to seek out and kill the offspring of another species, especially when they know that animal will hunt it one day."

"Survival of the fittest."

"Exactly."

Sasha followed Dayo over to a ramp that led up into the bed of a transport vehicle that had high railings on each side.

The big cat hesitated.

Then came the sound of her cub mewling as it appeared at the edge of the tailgate and looked down at its mother.

Sasha lumbered up the ramp and licked her cub. They moved toward the back of the cab of the truck and sprawled on the floor, the playful cub and the lioness happy to be reunited.

"Let's take Sasha and her cub home," Dr. Tomie said and they all climbed into the truck.

8

Adanna was the first to see the vultures circling high over the grassy plain. She knew the scavenger birds had keen eyesight and, from the air could spot a dead animal from two miles away. She counted more than twenty birds in the air, which meant that there was something big drawing their attention.

Isoba saw them, too. He cranked the wheel to avoid a deep ditch but kept his foot pressed down on the gas pedal, keeping the speedometer needle pegged at thirty.

They had been driving for almost an hour.

A small pack of wild dogs was up ahead, congregated near a patch of mesquite.

They had large ears and long, thin legs. The size of German shepherds, their coats were a patchwork of black and brown. Isola knew they were skilled hunters and would often split up into groups while chasing small impalas. The wild dogs were compassionate with their own kind, letting the feeble eat before the others.

Isoba sounded the horn and they scattered.

He stuck his head out the window and looked up. They were almost directly under the hovering funnel of birds, so he stopped the truck. He turned off the engine and climbed out.

Adanna reached back, opened the door for Samson, and the dog leaped out.

She grabbed a pair of binoculars and got out of the truck. She climbed up on the roof of the cab and did a complete sweep of the area with the binoculars.

"See anything?" Isola asked.

"No vehicles." Adanna hopped off the roof onto the bed and jumped down on the ground.

Isola reached inside the cab and took out his rifle.

Samson bounded over to the spot where the wild dogs had been gathered. He let out a forceful bark.

Isola and Adanna rushed over and came to an abrupt halt.

They were shocked at the brutality, no matter how often they saw it—and it was becoming more frequent. The rhino's head had been savagely mutilated, leaving a massive open wound where the face had once been.

Lying on the blood-soaked ground, the big gray looked to be about four tons.

Isola and Adanna were standing by the herbivore's back when they heard a high keening sound. Samson ran around the front legs of the rhino and stared at the underbelly.

Again, there was the same high-pitched cry.

Isola stepped around the rear of the fallen rhino while Adanna approached from the other side. As they came around the carcass, they saw something move. It was pressed against the dead rhino's belly.

A baby rhino. Refusing to leave its dead mother's side.

9

Dr. Tomie, Dayo, and Ally watched from the truck as Sasha and her cub ambled down the sloping knoll to an open area surrounded by boulders under a few umbrella-shaped acacia trees. A pride of lions was sharing the shade to escape the broiling sun.

"That's her family down there," Dr. Tomie said.

"How many are there?" Ally asked.

Dr. Tomie looked over at Dayo. "Last time we counted, twelve?"

"Yes," Dayo confirmed. "Three males, five lionesses, two little ones, and Sasha and her cub."

"They look pretty relaxed," Ally said.

"They're somewhat lazy when they're not hunting," Dayo said.

The three thick-maned lions watched Sasha intently as she strolled out of the sun and found her place in the shade. Her cub curled up against her chest. The other lionesses gave her a glance then shut their eyes. Two other cubs were play fighting in the grass despite the torrid heat.

"From up here, they look so peaceful, like a bunch of housecats," Ally said.

"Maybe so..."

The radio speaker on the dashboard crackled with a man's voice. "Dr. Tomie?"

Grabbing the mike from its holder, the veterinarian answered, "Yes, Isoba."

"Are you out in the field?"

"Yes, we've just returned Sasha and her cub back to her pride."

"Then you are not far from us. We are five miles to the east."

"We'll be there shortly," Dr. Tomie replied. She hung up the mike and started up the truck.

As they headed across the open plain, following the compass mounted on the dashboard, Ally had an opportunity to see large herds of zebras and wildebeest grazing on the grassland. She saw giraffes standing under the acacia trees, nibbling the leaves on the tall branches.

Isboa and Adanna were waiting by their truck when they arrived. Dr. Tomie pulled up and turned off the engine. She climbed out of the cab. Ally and Dayo got out as well and walked over.

"This way," Isoba said and took them around an entanglement of mesquite.

"Oh my God," Ally gasped when she saw the disfigured rhino lying on the ground.

"Dayo, go fetch a tarp," Dr. Tomie said. The woman ran back to the truck and, a moment later, returned with a folded white tarpaulin. Dr.

Tomie and Dayo shook out the canvas and covered the head of the rhino as a show of respect.

"Did an animal do that?" Ally asked.

"Poachers," Adanna said with disdain, like the word tasted foul when she spoke it.

"But why?" Ally thought she might cry but remained strong.

"On the black market, a rhino's horn goes for $60,000 a kilogram—which is more than gold," Dr. Tomie said.

"But for what?"

"The horn is ground up and sold as an aphrodisiac, mostly in Asia."

"But aren't there laws to stop it?" Ally asked.

"Yes, but they are hard to enforce. Elephants are still being killed today for their tusks even though there is a ban on the ivory trade."

Adanna looked down at the dead rhino. "This animal was killed just so an impotent man could get an erection."

"Adanna!" Isoba said sternly.

"It is true. Africa suffers just so the rich can pleasure themselves."

"I know how it upsets you," Isoba said to Adanna, "but let's not forget why we asked Dr. Tomie to come here."

Adanna motioned for everyone to come around to the other side of the dead rhino.

"Oh my," Ally said when she saw the baby rhino.

"She is sleeping," Isoba said. "We thought you could take her back."

"We'll take it from here," Dr. Tomie said. "You and Adanna go and see if you can track the poachers. Hopefully they're headed for the national park and we can alert the park rangers."

Isoba and Adanna rushed over, jumped into their truck, and raced off.

Dr. Tomie, Ally, and Dayo stood by and watched as the baby rhino slept.

"How much do you think she weighs?" Ally asked.

"I'd say around one fifty," Dr. Tomie said. "Let's wake her up and get her up on her feet."

Dayo had gone to the truck and returned with a long pole with a noose on the end.

"Are you afraid she'll run off?" Ally said once she saw the snare.

"Quite the opposite. We might have a problem getting her to leave her mother."

Dayo patted the baby rhino on the shoulder and the animal abruptly woke up. As soon as it opened its eyes it began to cry out. The young woman braced herself and lifted the animal up.

The baby rhino stood. Its large head was a third of its body length. The ears stood straight up. Its oversized feet looked almost comical and too big for its legs.

Dayo looped the noose around the baby rhino's head and pulled. The animal refused to budge.

"Looks like we might have to push," Dr. Tomie said.

Ally joined the doctor and they both got behind the reluctant rhino and guided it toward the back of the truck. It took the three of them to lift the baby rhino onto the bed.

"Why don't you two sit in the back and keep her company," Dr. Tomie said.

Dayo jumped up first, then Ally climbed into the back of the truck.

Dr. Tomie closed the tailgate and walked around to the driver's door. She got in and they started back to the clinic.

It was a jostling ride in the back, so Ally and Dayo had to hold onto the side railing while making sure the baby rhino didn't fall and get hurt.

"You're okay," Ally said, doing her best to steady the animal. "No one is going to hurt you." The baby rhino leaned against Ally. She looked over at Dayo.

"She thinks you are her new mother." Dayo grinned.

"Can I give her a name?"

"Sure. She will be with us for quite some time."

"Okay. How about... Lucy?"

"Lucy it is."

"Don't worry, Lucy, I'll take good care of you," Ally promised, putting her arm around Lucy's thick neck and giving the baby rhino an affectionate squeeze.

"Believe me, you will have your hands full," Dayo said.

10

While his stepfather and mother went back to their cottage to freshen up and change, Ryan took Dillon over to the dining room for something to eat. When they walked inside, Ryan was expecting a formal setting with linen tablecloths, not picnic tables with attached benches. It looked more like a military mess hall.

The kitchen was just on the other side of a serving counter. He could see skillets and pans hanging from hooks and heavy cast-iron pots on a low shelf. A large surface for frying food was next to a six-burner stovetop, along with two ovens. The room smelled of spices and fried grease.

A young woman with red hair pulled back in a braid stood behind the counter. Her back was turned, and she hadn't heard Ryan and Dillon come in.

"Excuse me," Ryan said.

The woman turned and smiled. "Oh, hello there."

"Could we get a couple sandwiches?"

"I'm sure you can," she replied and turned back to what she was doing.

"Let's go have a seat," Ryan said to Dillon. They sat down at the closest table and slid their legs over the bench. "What do you want?"

"A corndog."

"I doubt if they have those. How about a meat and cheese sandwich? I'm sure they've got that."

"No meat. Cheese," Dillon said.

"All right." Ryan looked up to place their order but the woman was no longer behind the counter.

She had come around and was sitting at one of the tables. She had prepared herself a steaming bowl of stew, along with a plate of bread. She dipped in her spoon and took a sip of broth.

"Ah, excuse me?" Ryan called over.

The woman looked up from her bowl. "Yes?"

"We're ready to order."

"That's nice," she replied and went back to eating her meal.

Dillon looked up at Ryan. "She's rude."

"I'll say."

The woman must have overheard their exchange because she glanced over. "Just so you know, I don't work here. I'm a guest. Just like yourselves."

"So what are you doing in the kitchen?"

"Dr. Tomie lets everyone pretty much help themselves. I guess she never told you."

"No, she didn't," Ryan said.

The woman slid off her bench and came over to Ryan and Dillon's table. "I'm sorry for the misunderstanding. I'm Celeste Starr." She held out her hand. Ryan shook her hand and introduced himself and Dillon.

"That's a cool name," Dillon said. "Are you an astronomer?"

"Dillon's just trying to be funny," Ryan apologized for his little brother.

"Actually, I am."

"Seriously?"

"I don't know what my parents were thinking. Strange how things happen."

"So, you're on vacation?" Ryan asked.

"No, I'm here for the meteor shower."

"What, from outer space?" Dillon asked.

"That's right. It's a project I've been working on. I don't know if you heard about it on the news, but each year for the past three years, Earth's been passing through an asteroid belt. Many scientists believe that the debris originated from Mercury. Right now, we're orbiting through it again. And if my calculations are correct, a meteorite should land near here. Then I can hopefully get a sample and prove their theory."

"Can we eat now?" Dillon asked impatiently.

"Dillon has a short attention span when he's hungry."

"Here, let me show you around the kitchen," Celeste said. "There's actually some more stew if you're interested. It's a little spicy but it's good."

"Is there any cheese? Dillon wanted a cheese sandwich."

"Hope he likes goat cheese."

11

Dr. Tomie pulled the truck into the yard and Gatura closed the gate. He went around to the back of the truck.

"What do we have here?" he said, once he saw Ally and Dayo sitting with the baby rhino.

"Poachers killed her mother," Dayo said.

The baby rhino made a loud *mmwonk* sound.

"Is she okay?" Ally asked.

"Even though she's lost her mother, she's happy you are her new one," Dayo said.

"Let me help you get her down," Gatura said. They were able to lift the heavy animal to the ground without startling her. Sensing her freedom, the baby rhino immediately ran around in circles then fell over in her excitement.

Ally rushed over. "I don't think she's too sure on her feet."

Lucy pushed herself off the ground with her thick legs.

Dr. Tomie walked over to the rear door of the clinic. She opened the door and stepped aside as Ryan and Dillon came out, and then she went inside.

As soon as Dillon saw Lucy, he yelled excitedly and ran over. "Is that a rhinoceros?"

"Sure is," Ally said.

"But it's so small."

"That's because it's a baby. Her name is Lucy."

"Can I play with her?"

"Well, first, I think she might be hungry."

"I had a crummy cheese sandwich. It was yuck."

Dayo had ducked into the building and returned with a large baby bottle from a stock of formula that Dr. Tomie used to wean other orphans.

She walked over to Ally. "Try her with this."

Ally took the bottle and offered the nipple to Lucy. The baby rhino took to the formula right away and began suckling. In a few minutes, the bottle was empty. "How much milk will she need?" Ally asked Dayo.

"About a gallon."

"Are you serious?"

"That's a gallon, five times a day," Dayo said.

"Oh my."

"Not to mention baths."

"You mean I'm going to have to get her into a bathtub?" Ally asked.

"No. Gatura will show you."

Gatura opened the gate on a stall and motioned for Ally to guide Lucy into the enclosure while Ryan and Dillon stood outside and watched. Once the animal was inside, Gatura closed the gate. He picked up a short length of hose that was attached to a faucet and turned on the water.

But instead of spraying Lucy, he just let the water puddle on the dirt into mud. After a moment, he turned off the water.

"Now she is ready for her bath."

"You mean... mud bath?"

"It will protect her from the sun and keep away the bugs."

Lucy didn't need any coaxing. She stepped into the middle of the puddle, lay down, and wallowed in the mud.

"And it will cool her down," Dayo said. "Be sure to get it all over her body."

"I'm doing it?"

"That's right."

Ally looked over at Dillon. "Want to give me a hand?"

"Sure," her little brother replied.

Ally reached down, picked up a handful of mud, and began slathering it onto Lucy's thick hide. Gatura opened the gate and let Dillon in. The boy grabbed a bunch of mud and spread it on the baby rhino.

Soon, Ryan couldn't help but start laughing. Then Gatura and Dayo joined in.

They couldn't tell who was covered in mud more: Lucy, or Ally and Dillon.

12

Isoba stopped the truck and climbed out of the cab. He walked ahead for a few paces and studied the tire tracks on the ground. In between the tread markings was a large rock that was chipped and covered with a black fluid. Isoba smiled when he saw the steady trail of oil leading away.

He looked over his shoulder and yelled, "We are in luck. They hit the oil pan."

Adanna got out of the truck and opened the rear passenger door so Samson could jump out. She went over to her father and stared at the rutted ground.

"They are following a small elephant herd," Isoba said.

She saw the line of oil. "Nice, they should show us the way."

Isoba looked at the horizon to the west and saw the sweltering sun dissolving behind a distant mountain ridge. "It will be dark soon."

"They will be easy to track."

"True, but there is a greater chance of an ambush. We will have to be careful," Isoba said then stood and looked around when he heard Samson barking.

"He's over by those trees," Adanna said.

Isoba and Adanna walked past the truck and over to a stand of acacia trees at the base of a hillock.

Samson was standing in front of a round boulder that stood over ten feet high. His head was down and his hackles were up and he was growling.

"There must be something behind that..." Isoba stopped when he saw the giant boulder move in their direction.

Samson kept snarling.

"That's not a rock. It's a giant dung ball," Adanna said, once the smell hit her.

Isoba reached down and grabbed Samson's collar to pull him back.

They moved out of the path of the revolving sphere of excrement and went behind a tree trunk to watch. Isoba knelt and held Samson tight against his body to quiet the agitated dog.

"That cannot be real," Adanna said as the behemoth globe rolled slowly by.

A giant dung beetle—the size of a Volkswagen—was pushing it along. The scarab was walking upside down on its front legs, shoving and spinning the dung ball with its four other legs.

Dung beetles, normally only an inch long, played a critical role burying and consuming animal waste, which improved the soil and reduced flies. A one-inch long dung beetle was capable of rolling a dung ball ten times its own weight.

This gigantic dung ball had to easily weigh a ton.

Isoba waited until the enormous dung beetle was far enough away before easing up on Samson's collar but still holding tight so the dog would not bolt after the giant insect.

"How is that possible?" Adanna asked her father.

"I don't know." He looked at the ground and spotted another dung beetle, but it was tiny, pushing a dung ball the size of a grape into a burrow. "Look, there's another one, but it is normal."

"I don't understand," Adanna said. "How did the other one get so big?"

"I have no idea," Isoba told his daughter. "We should go."

By the time they returned to the truck, the sun was already behind the mountains.

Isoba let Samson jump up front, and Adanna got behind the wheel. She started the engine, turned on the headlights, and the spotlights mounted on the roof of the cab.

Isoba climbed up onto the truck bed and aimed his rifle over the roof. Soon they would catch up to the poachers and pay them back for what they had done.

13

Frank and Wanda sat out on the deck chairs and watched the sunset. The view of the savanna was breathtaking as the landscape turned burnt orange and the bruising sky darkened the surface on the small lake just down the hill. As darkness approached, they could hear the distant roaring of lions, which seemed to carry for miles.

Ryan had recommended they try a spicy stew from the kitchen that was already made up. It proved to be a hearty meal with generous strips of guinea hen, tomatoes, and bell peppers floating in a thick, savory broth.

Frank had opened the complimentary bottle of wine that Dr. Tomie had left in their room. He took a sip and placed his glass on the little table between him and Wanda.

"So, how was your first day?" Frank asked.

"Didn't do much," Wanda replied and drank some of her wine.

"It's called *relaxing*."

"Oh, is that what it's called. I think poor Ally could use some of that. Did you see her and Dillon?"

"They were quite the pair," Frank smiled. "Taking care of Lucy is going to turn out to be quite the chore."

"I'll say. It's not even nine o'clock and I think she already turned in."

"Hey, Mom, can we join you?"

Wanda turned around in her chair and saw Ryan walking across the deck with a young woman.

"Well, hello."

"This is Celeste Starr," Ryan said, making the introduction. "She's also a guest here."

"Would you care for some wine?"

"No, thanks," Celeste said. She stood and looked up into the night sky.

"Please, sit down," Wanda said, waving her hand at two vacant lounge chairs.

"So are you a friend of Dr. Tomie?" Frank asked.

"No, not exactly," Celeste said. "I sent her an email asking if she didn't mind if I came out and stayed at her reserve so I could conduct my research."

"And what kind of research is that?"

"Celeste came here to watch a meteor shower," Ryan said.

"That's right," Celeste confirmed. "Tonight should be quite a show."

"So you're an astronomer?" Frank asked.

"That's correct."

"So why come to Africa? Couldn't you have seen this better from an observatory?"

"Actually, I'm here because I have it on good authority that some of the meteorites might have landed here on the reserve."

"That's a lot of area to cover," Wanda said.

"I know, but it beats traipsing through the jungle."

"What do you mean?"

"There have been similar meteor showers over the Amazon region"

"Hey, look, there's one now," Ryan said, pointing up at the green flash streaking across the night sky.

"There's another one," Wanda said.

"Jesus, will you look at that," Frank said.

A multitude of meteors trail across the black canvas like emerald tracer bullets. The show lasted for a good two minutes before it stopped.

"So how many was that?" Wanda asked. "Was anyone keeping count?"

"I was," Celeste said. "Twenty-seven."

14

Isoba was worried if they traveled throughout the night they would become too exhausted and decided Adanna and he should sleep in the truck. They awoke two hours before sunrise to continue their search. Adanna was driving when Isoba pounded on the roof. Adanna stopped the truck. She stuck her head out the window. "What is it?"

"Shut off the engine and turn out the lights."

Adanna turned off the ignition, the headlamps, and auxiliary lights. A green striate of light reflected off the windshield. "What was that?" she called out to her father.

"A shooting star, I think." He looked up and saw more flashes, glinting through the night sky. He heard a loud whoosh and ducked as a green fiery ball flew over the truck and sped off into the darkness. A few seconds later, he heard an impact, and saw a brief burst of emerald light in the distance.

Samson started barking and Adanna told him to be quiet.

Isoba looked up expecting to see more of the strange fireballs but instead he saw only the white pinpricks of the glimmering stars.

He pounded the roof and Adanna started up the truck. The headlamps came on and illuminated the stretch up ahead. Adanna put the transmission into gear and the vehicle moved forward.

They hadn't gone far when they came upon the poachers' abandoned truck. The doors had been left wide open. A tarpaulin covered a portion of the wood-railed flatbed.

Stopping, Adanna reached out and snapped on the searchlight mounted on the driver's door. She swiveled the lamp, casting a broad beam over the truck, then the nearby terrain.

Isoba saw something big and black dart out from behind a tall bush and skitter behind a dirt mound. It was the size of a Cape buffalo but moved too fast to be a bovine.

"Careful," Isoba called down to his daughter. "This may be a trap."

That's when the tarp flung back and three men began firing their rifles. Bullets pocked the windshield and Adanna slid down on the bench seat, pushing Samson down onto the floorboard.

Keeping her head down, Adanna reached out and swung the spotlight back at the attackers' truck, blinding the poachers.

Isoba took quick aim and picked each man off with his high-power rifle until they were lying in a lifeless heap.

Four more men stepped out from behind the bushes and began shooting. They wasted no time and rushed the truck.

Isoba had only one cartridge left in the chamber. With Adanna pinned down in the cab, he knew their chances of getting out alive were slim to none. He readied himself and took aim on the closest man.

Suddenly, the man stopped and screamed, dropping his gun and clutching his face. The other men screamed as well and dropped to their knees. They rolled on the ground into the beam of the spotlight.

Isoba could see the skin bubbling off of their faces and hands as they continued to wail in pain.

And then the creatures came into the light. There were three of them. They had red heads and legs, and their black bodies were massive.

Isoba couldn't believe his eyes.

They were giant bombardier beetles, the size of cows.

Steady streams of scalding liquid jetted from their anuses, dousing the four men withering on the ground. Steam rose off their bodies.

Isoba was relieved when the monstrous insects scampered away.

Another man who had been hiding in the front of the poachers' truck jumped out of the passenger side. He took one good look at the other unfortunate men and started running toward Isoba's vehicle.

Isoba vaulted down and clobbered the man, knocking him to the ground. Kneeling over the felled man, Isoba recognized him immediately with a thrill of triumph.

It was Duna.

Finally, they had the vile boss man that had been leading the slaughter of animals on the reserve. Before the man could speak, Isoba knocked him out with the butt of his rifle. He hoisted the man on his shoulder and tossed him onto the back of the truck. He climbed up and thumped the roof of the cab.

"Get us out of here."

Adanna backed up the truck, turned around, and they headed off into the darkness.

15

"What's that expression? All work and no play makes Jack a dull boy." Dr. Tomie sat behind the wheel of the open-air safari Jeep. It was only a few minutes before nine in the morning and it was already sultry.

"I believe that's right," Frank said, sitting in the front passenger seat. He looked over his shoulder. "You guys comfortable enough?"

Dr. Tomie hit a rut and the big Jeep took a hard bounce.

Wanda grabbed the railing on the back of the bench seat in front of her where Dillon and Ally were strapped in. Dillon was wearing a green baseball cap with the wildlife reserve's logo.

"Sorry about that," the doctor apologized. "As you can see, I'm not much of a driver. But I promise not to kill anyone."

Wanda grimaced but didn't say anything.

For the next fifteen minutes, Dr. Tomie drove over the savanna, stirring up herds of wildebeest and antelope. The animals wisely bolted out of her way as she drove through their masses.

"They don't like my driving either," the doctor laughed.

She slowed the safari Jeep and stopped so everyone could watch a group of giraffes standing under a mushroom-shaped tree. The longneck twenty-foot tall animals extended their purple tongues to strip leaves off of the thorny branches.

"Survival is key out here," Dr. Tomie said. "Even the plants have learned to adapt. See the tree those giraffes are feeding on? That's an acacia. The tree actually produces chemicals that make the leaves taste bad."

"So why do these giraffes keep eating them?" Ally asked.

"Giraffes don't eat their food right away. They generally swallow and store it in their stomachs in the event they have to run off to escape a predator. Later they regurgitate, much like a cow, and chew their cud."

"Hard to believe a tree can develop a defense system," Ally said.

"They can also lure stinging ants with a nectar as another deterrent against grazers."

"Symbiotic behavior," Ally said.

"Exactly," Dr. Tomie said. "Or in this case, mutualism. A good example would be the oxpecker. It's a small bird that can be seen perched on buffalos. The bovines tolerate the fowl as the oxpecker rids the buffalo of pests like ticks and mites."

"Uh-oh," Dillon said when one of the giraffes walked out from under the tree and started to approach the Jeep.

The giraffe strode over on its long legs and stopped just short of the vehicle.

Everyone gazed up at the towering animal.

It looked down and lowered its knobbed head.

The tip of its purple, twenty-inch long tongue wrapped around the bill of Dillon's cap and snatched it off the boy's head.

"Hey! Give that back," Dillon yelled.

Everyone broke out laughing as the giraffe turned and ambled back to the tree.

Dr. Tomie gunned the Jeep and they raced across the plain.

16

Dr. Tomie parked on a summit that provided an encompassing view of the grassy plains below. She pointed to a cheetah two hundred feet away, which was hiding in the taller sedge, watching a small herd of Thompson gazelles graze.

"Everyone please keep your voices down," the doctor whispered. "And we just might see this cheetah in action."

"How fast can they run?" Ryan asked.

"They can get to seventy miles an hour in four seconds."

"That's faster than my Trans Am."

"But they can only keep up that speed for a few hundred yards and then they're exhausted."

"Guess they burn up a lot of calories," Wanda said.

"I imagine they do," Dr. Tomie said. "But they also get overheated and can't eat their prey right away as they have to rest. Which means other predators can steal their kill."

"But won't the cheetah fight back?" Ally asked.

"Even though they are swift hunters, cheetahs are also timid. They generally shy away from bigger predators."

"What about their babies?" Dillon asked. "Don't they protect them?"

"That's a good question," Frank said.

"Yes, it is," the doctor agreed. "The cheetah is a good mother and will protect her cub or cubs to the death, if necessary. They are also great teachers. I've witnessed a mother teaching her cub to chase down a small impala. Each time the cub failed to bring the prey down, the mother would run after it and bring it back so the cub could give it another try."

"I think it's beginning," Frank said, pointing down the incline.

The cheetah stayed low and crept through the grass. As the big spotted cat approached, the antelopes must have sensed they were being stalked because they suddenly bolted off.

Bounding after the herd, the cheetah's unbelievably long stride enabled it to quickly catch up to the fleeing animals. One of the gazelles darted away from the herd and the sleek cat was right on its tail. The two-pronged gazelle ran zigzag, but the cheetah shadowed its every movement and grabbed a hind leg with its sharp claws, pulling the animal down.

Wanda turned to shield Dillon's eyes just as the cheetah sunk its sharp teeth into the gazelle's throat.

"Mom!" Dillon protested. "They show this stuff all the time."

Wanda looked over at Frank.

He shrugged. "Not my fault he likes the Discovery Channel."

"And who got him hooked on that?" Wanda wanted to know.

Luckily, Dr. Tomie intervened by saying, "Life can seem harsh out here but it's nature's way."

"I guess humans aren't that different," Wanda said. "Seems like everyone's always wanting to get at the top of the food chain."

"Aren't you the profound one," Frank quipped.

"Preservation is a key element in these animals' survival. Some species purposely go out of their way to kill a predator's young so the infant won't someday be hunting them."

"But how would they know?" Wanda asked.

"I believe it's coded in their DNA."

"Hey, look!" Ryan said, directing everyone's attention to the two male lions wandering over to where the cheetah lay with the slain gazelle.

"Are those two from Sasha's pride?" Ally asked.

"I do believe they are," Dr. Tomie confirmed.

"Oh boy," Dillon said. "A fight!"

Dr. Tomie glanced over her shoulder and saw the concerned look on Wanda's face. "Perhaps we should get back to the clinic. I have an ostrich that is in very need of an enucleation."

"What's that?" Dillon asked.

"You don't want to know," Ally said.

"Sure I do," Dillon insisted.

"It means I'm going to have to remove an eye," Dr. Tomie said.

"What?" Dillon said.

"The eye is badly infected, I'm afraid. If I don't perform the surgery, the bird will die. Besides, she's already blind in that eye, so it is of no use."

"That's the one we saw out in the corral," Ryan said.

"That's right. Perhaps when we get back, someone would like to assist while we get her ready for pre-op."

"Sure, I will," Ally said. She looked over at her mom.

"I can help as well," Wanda said.

"Great," Dr. Tomie said. "Okay, everyone, hold on to your hats." She started the engine, turned the Jeep around, and they raced down the opposite side of the declivity away from the cheetah and the bullying lions.

17

Dr. Tomie parked the Jeep behind the clinic and everyone got out. Frank decided he would take Ryan and Dillon over to the kitchen and throw together a late breakfast while Wanda and Ally helped the doctor prepare for surgery.

"As you are familiar with firearms, Wanda, let me show you how to prepare a tranquilizer dart," Dr. Tomie said as they entered the supply room.

The doctor opened a cabinet door and took out a small bottle of clear liquid. She pulled open a drawer and grabbed the component parts for the dart, which she placed on a table next to the small bottle. She opened a booklet and fanned through the pages until she found the page that showed the proper dosage required to sedate the 300-pound ostrich.

"First, we remove the cap on our barbiturate, then we insert the hypodermic needle in and draw the liquid into the syringe," Dr. Tomie said as Wanda and Ally watched. Once the syringe was filled to the correct cubic centimeter, the doctor pulled out the needle and recapped the bottle. "Now, we insert the hypo into the dart housing and twist it shut."

She went over and unlocked a metal cabinet. Reaching inside, she took out a tranquilizer gun: a slighter version of a long-barreled rifle with a handgrip and ten-inch metal stock. It was also equipped with a mounted riflescope for precise aiming.

After Dr. Tomie loaded the dart with the sedative syringe, she handed the rifle to Wanda.

Dayo came into the room. "I've boiled and laid out your instruments."

"Good. Take Ally with you and give her a brief rundown so she will be prepared once we start surgery."

"Very well," Dayo replied. She smiled at Ally and they both walked out into the hall. Dr. Tomie and Wanda went out through the back entrance.

"I'll have Gatura wrangle the ostrich while you prepare your shot," Dr. Tomie instructed. She signaled to Gatura—who was shoveling dung out of Lucy's enclosure—to come and join them. He walked over to where the doctor and Wanda were standing just outside the ostrich's corral.

The highest railing was just over six feet tall. The ostrich's head was two feet above that.

"Be careful and don't get kicked," the doctor warned Gatura.

"I will. She is half-blind, so there is no worry."

"Then I'm going to run inside and see if Dayo has everything prepped. I'll be back shortly," Dr. Tomie said and went into the building.

Gatura opened the gate slowly while Wanda went over and set the barrel of the tranquilizer rifle on a lower railing so that she could set up the shot.

The ostrich was turned the other way, looking out at the savanna, no doubt wishing it were out there running free instead of cooped up in the corral. Gatura was five feet inside the enclosure when the large bird suddenly turned around. It took one look at Gatura, fluffed its large wings, and charged.

"Look out!" Wanda yelled and fired the rifle. The projectile hit the ostrich in the side but the sedative didn't immediately take effect. The ostrich ran up and knocked Gatura down and began kicking the man with its powerful legs, the two-toed feet pummeling the man where he lay.

Wanda dropped the rifle and bolted into the corral. She waved her arms and yelled, "Get back," thinking she could reason with the giant bird like she would with her English bull terrier, Winston, back home.

She ran up to push the bird away. The ostrich turned and glared at her with its good eye, and before Wanda knew what was happening, the bird snapped its long neck forward and pecked her in the shoulder. It hurt like hell but it wasn't enough to stop her from trying to get to Gatura. She crouched over Gatura to protect him.

The ostrich blindsided Wanda and kicked her in the shoulder.

This time, the pain was so intense, she passed out.

18

Rather than try to cook something up in the kitchen, Frank opted they should have a fast breakfast of cereal. He found a couple boxes with unfamiliar brand names on a shelf that contained frosted flakes and strawberry rice crunches. After grabbing three bowls and spoons, he divvied out portions and added goat's milk. He ate his, Ryan only finished half his bowl, and Dillon put his spoon down after the first bite.

"Doesn't taste right," Dillon griped.

Frank half expected Dillon to spit out his first bite, but he hadn't. He pushed a bowl of fruit across the table toward the boy. "Here, eat a banana."

Dillon made a face but took a banana anyway and began peeling back the skin.

A few minutes later, after cleaning up after themselves, Ryan and Dillon wanted to go back to their cottage. Frank said sure and they went their separate ways.

Frank strolled over to the clinic and went inside. He followed the main corridor to the rear of the building and stepped out into the animal compound.

That's when he saw the ostrich lying on its side in the dirt. He approached cautiously and saw a green tuft sticking out of the giant bird's black-feathered side—a tranquilizer dart.

Looking around, he spotted the open gate to one of the pens.

"Oh my God," he said, once he saw Wanda, then Gatura, both sprawled on the ground. He rushed over to his wife and knelt in the dirt. "Wanda, are you all right?"

Slowly, she opened her eyes. "Be careful, there's a..." but then she grimaced when she tried to move.

"Did the ostrich do this?"

She managed to nod her head.

Frank heard a moan and glanced over at Gatura. The man was struggling to get up. As soon as he stood, he began to hobble on one leg.

"Gatura, are you okay?" Frank asked.

"I got kicked good," Gatura said with a weak smile. He looked down and saw Wanda. "I'll go get Dr. Tomie." Even though Gatura had trouble walking, he still managed to limp quickly over to the rear door of the building.

In less than a minute, Dr. Tomie was running out the door. Dayo and Ally were right behind, carrying a canvas stretcher.

"Mom!" Ally shouted when she saw her mother lying on the ground.

Dr. Tomie knelt next to Frank and looked down at Wanda. "Where are you hurt?"

Wanda raised her right hand and pointed to her left shoulder.

The doctor touched the spot gently and got an immediate response when Wanda gasped a deep breath.

"She may have a broken clavicle. Let's get her onto the stretcher and bring her inside."

Dayo looked over at the ostrich lying on its side. "What about it?"

"Let's fix Wanda up first, then it will be the bird's turn," Dr. Tomie said.

***

"How serious is it?" Frank asked, standing next to Wanda sitting on the table.

"It will be uncomfortable for awhile, so I've administered some painkillers," Dr. Tomie said, as she finished with the figure-eight bandage that covered Wanda's shoulder and under her armpit. "The collarbone should knit on its own."

Frank helped Wanda with her shirt. Raising her left arm gingerly, he guided her arm into the sling he had placed over her head.

"How long do I have to wear this?" Wanda asked.

"Depends—everyone heals differently," Dr. Tomie said. "I would keep your arm immobile for a few weeks so as not to aggravate the break."

"We should cut this short and get you back home," Frank said.

"Nonsense," Wanda replied. "I don't want to be the one that botched up our vacation. And louse up Ally getting an opportunity to work with the doctor."

"On that note, I should go," Dr. Tomie said. "I have a sick bird to attend to."

"Thanks again," Wanda said as the veterinarian left the room.

"So, what now?" Frank asked.

"Looks like I'll have plenty of time to sit around and do nothing."

"I think the word you're looking for is *relaxing*."

Wanda winced as she got on her feet. "Sure. Be a dear and grab my meds."

19

It was sweltering sitting in the bed of the truck under the baking sun. Isoba had refused to take his eyes off of Duna for one moment. Adanna had even offered to switch places and guard the poacher boss man and let her father drive, but Isoba had insisted she would be more comfortable inside the truck. Samson's nose had left wet smudges on the glass of the cab's rear window as the dog kept a vigilant watch on the two men riding in the back.

"Why do you bother?" Duna taunted. "You know they will come for me."

"Not this time," Isoba said. "This time I will make sure you rot in jail—just like all those animals you killed."

Duna laughed. He was a burly man, bigger than Isoba, and had chestnut skin where Isoba's was darker, almost a chocolate. They were of different ancestral heritages and were occupational opposites. Their hatred for each other boiled in their blood.

"Weak words from a weak man," Duna grinned.

Isoba slammed the butt of his rifle stock across the man's cheek and wiped the smile off of Duna's face.

"Do not do that again," Duna warned, even though there wasn't much he could do about it. His hands were tied behind his back and his ankles were bound with rope.

"I am not afraid of you, Duna."

"No, but what about my men?"

"I saw your men killed, by those..."

"Demons?"

"I don't think that is what they were," Isoba said.

"Then what?"

"I don't know."

"My brother will come for me," Duna said, managing a grin, despite the welt on his cheek.

"Let him try." Isoba hated Duna's brother, Abrafo, even more than he loathed Duna.

Adanna stuck her head out the driver's window and yelled up, "There's a vehicle up on that ridge."

A new-model Land Rover was parked up near a stand of trees. Isoba grabbed a pair of binoculars and gazed up, hoping the vehicle belonged to a park ranger and he could hand Duna over to the authorities. He scanned the side of the four-wheeler but didn't see any emblems on the door. There were two occupants inside the off-road SUV: a black man in the driver's seat, and a large white man with a gray beard sitting in the passenger seat.

"Should I stop?" Adanna asked.

"No, keep driving," Isoba answered.

He put the binoculars down and turned his attention back to Duna.

For some strange reason Isoba couldn't stop thinking about the big man up in the Land Rover. He had seen him somewhere before but couldn't place the face.

20

Tyrone Vane kept a keen eye on the truck below as it drove away. For a minute, Vane was worried that the man observing them with the binoculars might signal the driver to head up the slope. If that had happened, Vane was ready for any altercation. He tucked his Desert Eagle .44 Magnum back into his shoulder holster and instructed his driver and guide, Gwala, to put away his gun.

"Did you recognize the truck?" Vane asked.

"Yes," Gwala said. "It is from the Tomie Reserve."

"Will they be a problem?"

"No, sir. There is only a father and daughter that patrol, and that was them."

"Good. This might prove easier than I thought. As long as we know where they are at all times, we can avoid detection."

Vane looked out through the passenger window. "Let's set up a day camp here for awhile and then we can go look for the pride."

"Yes, Mr. Vane." Gwala got out of the Land Rover and walked around to the back of the vehicle. He opened the cargo door.

The first task was to set up the outdoor surveillance system. Gwala strategically placed eight wireless infrared sensors hooked on mounting poles around the campsite. If any intruder—animal or human—were to pass through the invisible beams and break the connection, an ear-piercing alarm would be triggered.

Gwala took a couple minutes and erected a shade canopy between two trees. He then set up a chair and a small table.

He went over to the Land Rover and brought back a large cooler—personally packed by a master chef at the five-star hotel where Vane was staying—which he placed on the ground under the canopy. He opened the lid. Inside was a double magnum of Armand De Brignac Brut Rose champagne packed in dry ice along with specially prepared containers of smoked salmon, gourmet cheeses, artisan breads, chocolate-covered strawberries, and an assortment of delectable sweets.

During the time Gwala prepared the temporary day camp, Vane pensively smoked one of his cheroots while standing on a crest that overlooked the sprawling savanna...

Ruminating about the trophy white lioness.

21

Adanna drove around to the rear of the clinic and stopped the truck in front of the closed gate. She honked the horn for someone to let them in, expecting Gatura to come over, but he was nowhere to be seen, so she opened her door and climbed out of the cab.

Samson bolted out after her.

Walking over, she unlatched the gate and pushed it open. Samson raced into the compound. Adanna got back into the truck and drove into the compound. She parked in front of a stucco animal enclosure with a jail-like door.

Isoba pushed Duna down off the tailgate. The man fell to his knees as his feet were still bound. He scowled up at Isoba. "You are making a big mistake."

Isoba stood over Duna and pulled out his knife.

Duna's eyes grew wide as he stared at the blade glinting in the blazing sun.

Isoba pointed the sharp knife and leaned down. Duna tried to scoot back, only to fall on his side. The keen blade cut through the rope binding Duna's ankles.

"Get up," Isoba ordered, slipping his knife back in the sheath, and aiming his rifle at Duna's chest.

The boss man got to his feet.

Isoba stuck the muzzle of his rifle barrel into Duna's lower back and shoved the man forward. Adanna went over and opened the door with the jail-like bars. Once Duna was inside, Isoba told him to sit on the ground, and he tied the man's ankles.

Stepping out, Isoba closed the door and secured it with a large padlock.

He heard voices and turned.

Dr. Tomie stepped out through the rear doorway of the clinic. Frank and Wanda followed her. Isoba wondered why Wanda's arm was in a sling.

"We caught him and he is locked up," Adanna said to Dr. Tomie.

"You have Abrafo?"

"No, I'm sorry. It's Duna," Isoba said.

Dr. Tomie's face reddened with rage.

Frank looked at the angry doctor. "Gayle, are you okay?"

Instead of replying, she turned and stormed back to the rear door.

"Why did she get so upset?" Wanda said.

Isoba waited until the doctor went inside then said, "Duna and his brother, Abrafo, have been poaching our reserve and the national parks for years. They are evil men."

"And now you have one in custody," Wanda said. "Good for you."

"We can only hold Duna for the park rangers," Isoba said.

"But he'll do some serious prison time, right?"

"It is very doubtful," Adanna said.

"He has connections with very rich people in the black market," Isoba explained.

"So, you're saying he might not even go to trial."

"That is right."

"Duna and Abrafo are like slippery eels," Adanna sniped.

"Well, Dr. Tomie should be somewhat relieved," Frank said.

Isoba had a glum expression on his face. "I think she'd rather we had captured Abrafo."

"And why's that?" Frank asked.

Adanna looked at the door where Dr. Tomie had disappeared. "Abrafo killed her husband."

22

"Thank you for doing this," Dr. Tomie said. "Gatura is in no condition to walk back to his village."

"Well, I'm here to help out in any way I can," Frank said. He was sitting behind the large steering wheel of an old-model Willys Jeep that was no doubt a military issue leftover from the Second World War. He glanced over at Gatura, sitting up front in the passenger seat. "So how far is your village from here?"

"Ten miles," Gatura replied.

"You mean to tell me you walk that distance back and forth so you can help with the animals?"

"Yes, every day."

"In this heat?" Frank figured the temperature had to be one hundred ten degrees, if not more, and there was little or no shade on the savanna.

Gatura nodded.

"Gatura and the others are quite dedicated," Dr. Tomie said.

"If we do not save the animals," Gatura said. "Who will?"

Frank smiled and put a hand on Gatura's shoulder. "The world needs more people like yourself."

"Try and stay off the leg for a couple days," Dr. Tomie instructed Gatura.

"But what about tomorrow?"

"We'll manage," Dr. Tomie said, but when she saw the hurt look on Gatura's face, she added, "Heal quickly as the animals will miss you." That brightened Gatura's spirits as he gave her a smile.

They heard loud voices beyond the corral.

Ally, Dayo, and five other volunteers were cheering the one-eyed ostrich as it trotted away onto the prairie, having recuperated from its surgery.

Even though the ostrich was to blame for Gatura's injury, he too smiled, seeing the large bird returning back to the wild.

"Is it okay if we come along?" Ryan asked, approaching the Jeep. Celeste was with him, carrying a small black case.

"Sure, we have room," Frank said, pointing to the small bench seat butted up against the spare tire mounted over the rear bumper. He looked at Celeste's bag. "What do you have there?"

"Oh, I thought I'd bring my computer. As I've been tracking the meteor showers, I thought we might end up in the vicinity where one might have landed."

"Well, that might be a possibility." Frank glanced over at Ryan. "How's your mom doing?"

"She's lying down." Ryan boosted Celeste up so she could step into the back of the Jeep.

"Your wife is very brave," Gatura said to Frank.

"That she is," Frank said, somewhat saddened that she couldn't be with them. He looked over at Dr. Tomie. "Well, Gayle, I guess we're off."

"You should visit awhile when you get to the village," Dr. Tomie said. "I understand there is an event happening there that should interest you."

"Is that right," Frank said. He started the ignition, slipped the transmission into gear, and they headed out onto the sweltering flatland.

23

The village was only fourteen homes. Most of the dwellings were made of bleached-white mud, some with clay brickwork, and all were circular. The thatched roofs were low-pitched and conical with extending branches forming eaves.

Frank saw a large group of people congregated a hundred yards away from the outskirts of the village. The men, talking and sitting in a semicircle on the ground, wore loose-fitting button shirts and dust-covered trousers. The women's attire was quite the contrast to the men's drab garb, as the fabric of their long dresses was vibrant red, purple, green, blue, and just about every other color in the rainbow.

Everyone was gathered under the scorching sun despite half a dozen crudely set up lean-tos nearby.

"How come they're not in their homes?" Ryan asked, wiping the sweat from his brow.

"They do not want to be eaten," Gatura replied and smiled.

"Eaten? By what?" Celeste said.

"You will see."

Frank drove up and parked next to a makeshift livestock pen. Rocks had been piled up to form posts and crudely honed tree limbs served as railings. There were about a dozen sheep, but mostly the enclosure was packed with goats.

He scooted off the driver's seat and helped Celeste down from the rear seat. Gatura got out on his side and Ryan climbed down.

A few of the men greeted Gatura and he waved back. When he started to limp around the front of the Jeep, a tall woman in a canary yellow dress rushed over and put her hand on his arm.

"No worry. My leg will soon heal," Gatura said in their language and gave the woman a reassuring kiss on the cheek. The woman smiled and walked over to an area where some of the children were playing with the village dogs, while others kicked a soccer ball back and forth in the wretched heat.

Gatura hobbled over to one man standing next to a wire mesh coop. Inside were free-range chickens. Frank was surprised to see them in the coop; he'd thought they would be foraging for food around the village. Gatura exchanged a few words with the man before coming back and joining Frank, Ryan, and Celeste.

"They are almost done," Gatura said. "Please, this way, but watch where you step."

The first thing Frank noticed when they entered the village was the tiny skeletons everywhere: mostly rodents and birds. The bones had been picked clean.

"What in the world?" Celeste said.

Frank scanned the small carcasses and saw a large mass moving along the ground, down between two of the dwellings. "Here, this way."

As they got closer, Ryan said, "Are those ants?"

"Army ants, to be more concise," Frank said. "Looks like a migrating colony. They're often called the Mongol horde."

"And what, they just decided to march through these poor people's village?" Celeste said.

"It's not that bad," Gatura said. "The ants rid our village of pests, like cockroaches and rats."

"Actually, army ants consume everything in their path—vegetation, insects, animals, and even us if we don't get out of their way," Frank said. He looked down, spotted two specks on the ground, and bent over. He picked up the two stragglers and put them in the palm of his hand. He stood and showed Ryan and Celeste.

"The bigger ant is a soldier. Check out the ice-tong mandibles. They use those to serrate their prey. The other one is a worker ant. They carry food and serve the queen."

"You mean the queen ant is in this bunch?" Celeste asked.

"Sure, and heavily guarded. At night after a march, the soldiers will form a protective shield around the queen and her eggs with their bodies. A single queen can produce an entire colony."

"And how many ants is that?" Ryan asked.

"Could be twenty million."

"From just one queen?" Ryan said with astonishment.

"That's right. If you were to weigh all the ants in the world, they would weigh as much as all the humans on the planet. Remember, we're talking ten thousand trillion... Ouch!"

"What happened?" Celeste asked.

"The soldier bit me," Frank replied and brushed off his hands.

A woman let out a bloodcurdling scream.

"What the heck?" Celeste said.

Men began yelling joined by the bleating sheep and goats. Even the chickens were cackling.

"What's going on?" Frank said. He rushed toward the mayhem followed by Ryan and Celeste, with Gatura limping behind them.

As they got closer, Frank could see the horrified expressions on the villagers' faces as they backed away from the livestock pen.

Frank couldn't blame them when he saw what was attacking the livestock. Neither could Ryan and Celeste.

"What in the hell," Ryan blurted.

24

The army ant's pale-orange head was the size of a beach ball.

A small goat was impaled between the tips of the giant insect's mandibles, elevated a foot off the ground like a block of ice being carried by a pair of tongs. Crying and kicking, the goat struggled to get free, but the ant's appendages were too strong. The jaws closed, and the goat's abdomen ripped open. Blood and entrails spilled onto the heads and backs of the other livestock.

Four more ants were either climbing over the railing or coming around the other side of the corral. They were enormous. Their segmented bodies—the head, thorax, and gaster—had to be eight feet long. The ants stood on their long, spindly legs over the frightened livestock, as tall as any person in the village.

A railing was knocked over, collapsing a pile of stones when another ant entered the pen and attacked a ewe. The sheep fell on its back with its hooves in the air. The ant lowered its head and thrust its mandibles into the soft belly of the animal.

"We have to stop them," Frank yelled.

"But how?" Ryan asked. "We don't have guns."

"Maybe the villagers have weapons," Celeste said.

Gatura and two other men appeared with machetes they had retrieved from the dwellings.

Frank saw more men returning from their homes, each with a spear or what looked like a wooden pitchfork. It was obvious that they were not going to let their livestock be slaughtered without a fight.

A villager tried to thrust his spear into an ant's head, but the tip broke on the thick exoskeleton—about as useless as stabbing a football helmet with a pencil.

A man with a machete ran up to one of the ants and swung the blade, lopping off an antenna. The ant rushed the man and shoved him to the ground. It lowered its head and placed its mouthparts over the man's face. His muffled cry could be heard as the ant excreted a tissue-dissolving solution and sucked the man's liquefied flesh from his skull.

Frank ran over. He grabbed the machete off the ground. The ant was too busy feeding on the dead villager to notice Frank stepping around its flank.

Raising the machete over his head, Frank brought the blade down swiftly, and chopped through the narrow waist that connected the main body of the thorax to the gaster, the segment that housed the creature's stomachs and digestive system.

Green gunk spurted out of the gaster as it fell off onto the dirt and lay motionless.

Reacting to the pain of suddenly been cut in half, the ant raised its head and stepped off the dead man. It staggered on its six legs like a drunken circus performer on stilts as more life-sustaining fluids poured out of its wounded body.

One of the ants had trampled the coop and was attacking the chickens. The cackling birds were flapping their wings and colliding into one another trying to escape the huge ant snapping its mandibles like sickles and ripping apart the flock.

Frank heard the Jeep start up. He turned and saw Ryan behind the wheel, and Celeste sitting up front. Before he could call out to them, Ryan spun the four-wheel vehicle around the corral.

That's when Frank saw two of the giant ants chasing three brightly clad women, who were screaming as they ran.

One of the women fell.

She turned and gazed at the monstrous ants racing toward her.

The front grill of the Jeep smashed into the ants, sending one flying in the air and over Ryan and Celeste's heads as it landed on the ground. The other ant was crushed under the tires and squashed to death.

Ryan turned the Jeep around and raced toward the ant struggling to get up.

The quarter-ton vehicle mowed over the creature, snapping off legs and flattening its head with a loud *goosh!*

Frank saw Gatura and another man hacking away at one of the ants as it converged on them, but they were having little success in killing the thing.

"Gatura! Go for the petiole!"

Gatura shot Frank a puzzled look.

Frank pointed to his midsection. "The waist!"

Gatura said something to the other man, and they outflanked their heinous attacker, staying clear of the deadly mandibles and lunging with their machetes, cutting through the ant's narrow waist.

A group of men stood around the final ant they had collectively slain. The ground was littered with feathers and bloody chickens. Most of them were dead, some still twitching.

Frank walked over to the Jeep. "Nice work, Ryan," he said, complimenting his stepson for his quick thinking.

"Thanks. What now?"

Frank looked over at Gatura. "If you like, you can burn them. Just leave us one that we can take back and examine."

"Our people are afraid and think they are evil spirits," Gatura said. "Demons!"

"No, I'm afraid they're real."
"Do you think our village will be safe?"
"I wish I could say yes."

25

Tyrone Vane indulged in another flute of champagne and sat back in the folding chair under the canopy. He patted the belly of his shirt straining over the bulge over his belt, relishing his lavish meal. From where he sat, he could see across the great plains of the savanna, the magnificent view stretching as far as the naked eye could see.

He thought while he was whiling away the early afternoon, staying out of the blazing sun and escaping the hottest time of the day, he might take the opportunity to take the VO Falcon out of the case and familiarize himself with the prodigal hunting rifle.

"Gwala! Go fetch my..."

Vane sat erect when the surveillance alarm went off, chirping loudly. He stood and yanked the Desert Eagle out of the shoulder holster. He saw a green sensor light flashing on a post staked twenty feet from the encampment. Looking around, he saw more of the warning lights blinking, meaning that there was more than one intruder.

Gwala stood next to the Land Rover. He threw back the bolt on his rifle and proceeded to comb the inside perimeter of the camp.

Vane cocked back the hammer on his big handgun. The constant chirping was getting on his nerves. He picked up the key fob remote off the table and silenced the piercing noise with a push of a button. Now that it was quiet, he hoped to hear the interlopers.

There was something moving behind the off-road SUV parked fifteen feet away.

He dropped down to one knee so he could see under the vehicle. An animal scampered from behind the front tire and hid behind the rear tire.

"Gwala! There's one behind the truck!"

The guide ran over, aiming his rifle, but before he could get off a shot, the animal lunged out from behind the Land Rover.

Gwala screamed as the eighty-pound Chacma baboon slammed into his chest and knocked him to the ground. The gray monkey clawed the man's face and chomped down, ripping the man's throat out with its sharp teeth as it flung back its head, shaking blood everywhere.

Vane walked up on the carnage and fired his gun.

The high-caliber projectile riddled a hole clear through the baboon's skull, sending purple brain matter splashing onto the dirt.

Vane heard footfalls behind him and turned. Another baboon rushed him. He took careful aim and halted the animal with a bullet to the chest. The baboon tumbled and ended up facedown in the dirt only a foot away from Vane's boots.

A black insect the size of a dinner plate was attached to the baboon and looked like an absurd backpack with eight legs. The head was burrowed into the baboon's fur, the body bloated like a water balloon.

Vane aimed and blasted the giant tick. The ruptured body exploded in a bloody mist. He looked around, expecting another attack, but he didn't see any more baboons lurking about.

He held the big gun down by his side and walked over to Gwala. Even though the guide's eyes were wide open, the man was clearly dead. Blood continued to drain out of the savage wound and form a crimson pool in the dirt.

"Damn it to hell," Vane swore. He wasn't upset that Gwala was dead. Sure, he'd miss being chauffeured and having his own personal servant. What really irked him was that he would have to be the one having to perform the menial task of breaking camp and stowing everything in the Land Rover.

He decided there was no hurry and went back to his chair to wait out the heat and drink more champagne.

Hopefully he wouldn't have to deal with too many flies.

26

As there was only enough room in the Jeep for the four of them, Frank decided they would have to go back to the clinic and retrieve a larger vehicle. Turned out, Isoba was more than happy to help when they returned. Frank and Isoba made a trip out to the village in the flatbed truck and brought back the dead ant that Frank had killed earlier.

When they drove into the compound, a couple village volunteers were shocked when they saw the cargo. They watched nervously as Frank and Isoba got out of the vehicle and went around to the back of the truck.

Ryan was standing by to help as well. He shook out a large tarpaulin and placed it on the ground by the rear bumper.

Frank grabbed a leg and Isoba grabbed another, and they pulled the giant ant off the bed and let it fall onto the tarp.

Ryan reached up, put his arms around the severed gaster, and lifted it off the truck. "This has to weigh a good fifty pounds."

"Lay it on the tarp," Frank said. "I think the three of us can carry it in."

Ryan lowered the segment and rested it in between the enormous ant's gangly legs folded up against its body.

Isoba looked over at Adanna, who was seated just outside the animal enclosure where they were keeping Duna detained. She had been watching the men offload the giant ant. "Father, have you told them?" Adanna called out.

Frank looked at Isoba. "Told us what?"

"We did not mention it before because we thought you would think us crazy."

"What, you've seen the giant ants before?" Frank asked.

"No, not ants," Isoba said. "We saw a giant dung beetle."

"That is crazy," Ryan said, almost about to laugh.

Isoba scowled at the young man. "The night we captured Duna, his men were killed by bombardier beetles."

"I'm sorry," Ryan apologized. "When you said dung beetle..."

"I think what Ryan is trying to say is it's all too weird," Frank said in Ryan's defense. "Let's get this inside and see if we can make sense of all this."

It was a tight squeeze getting the cumbersome creature through the doorway and down the narrow corridor, but they finally managed to get to the examining room. They lifted the larger portion of the ant onto one table and put the gaster on a gurney covered with plastic.

Frank turned when Dr. Tomie and Dayo came into the room. The two women gaped at the creature on the table.

"Oh my Lord. I had no idea it would be this big," Dr. Tomie said. "Even after you described what happened at the village."

"Where're Wanda, Ally, and Dillon?" Frank asked.

"Over at the dining hall with Celeste." Dr. Tomie said.

"Okay. Where would you like to start?"

"You're the expert, you take the lead."

"Very well," Frank said. "Let's start with the gaster."

Dayo pushed a cart with a large tray of surgical tools over to the gurney.

Frank slipped on a purple pair of nitrile exam gloves. He reached into the tray and grabbed a scalpel. He attempted to make the first cut but the exoskeleton was too hard for the blade to penetrate. "I'm going to need a bone saw."

"There's one on the cart," Dayo said. She picked up the hand tool with the circular blade and handed it to Frank.

"Thanks." Frank pushed a button and applied the spinning blade. The tool made a loud grinding noise as he sawed through the length of the gaster. "Give me a hand and let's flip it over."

Dr. Tomie and Ryan, who had both donned gloves, picked up the gaster and rolled it onto its opposite side. Much of the internal fluids leaked out onto the plastic sheet, some even dripping onto the floor.

Frank started the saw and ran the whirling blade from one end to the other. Once he was through, he put the saw down. "Okay, let's pop this sucker open." He inserted his fingers in between the halved shells and pried the gaster apart so that they could examine the cross sections.

Three large, connected organs flopped onto the plastic.

"What is all that?" Ryan asked.

"Well, first of all you have to remember that ants cannot digest solid food. They actually excrete a chemical that liquifies their food. After they lap it up with their tongues, the liquid is stored in the crop. That's this here," Frank said, pointing to the organ that was closest to the severed end.

"How much do you think an insect this large could consume?" Dr. Tomie asked.

"Ants can be gluttons. I've seen a lab test where ants were allowed to drink as much sugar water as they wanted. Imagine a one-inch ant with a stomach the size of a Ping-Pong ball."

"So, what's this one do?" Ryan asked, pointing to the next organ.

"That's the midgut, where the ant gets its nutrients. The other organ is the rectum. I don't think I need to explain its function."

Frank reached down and carefully removed a foot-long spine with a sharp point and a small sack attached at the other end. "This is its stinger."

"What's that bag?" Ryan asked.

"That would be the poison gland."

"How poisonous do you think these things are?"

Frank held up the sack, which was the size of his fist. "I'd say there's enough venom here to kill an elephant."

27

Frank rubbed his hand over the ant's smooth head then tapped his knuckles on the polished exoskeleton. "It's like a hard plastic."

Dr. Tomie and Dayo stood on one side of the table and observed as Frank explained the ant's functions as though he were conducting one of his entomology classes back at UC Davis.

"Ants have what's called the ocellus, which means they have simple eyes much like ours and have only a single lens—unlike flies, which have compound eyes and multiple lenses."

"So do they have good eyesight?" Ryan asked.

"No, some ants are actually blind. By the looks of this one, I think its vision is blurry at best. I'd say it reacts to sudden movement."

"So, if you weren't to move, it wouldn't see you?"

"Well, not right away. Ants have a keen sense of smell. They can even use their antennae to sniff out food. Plus, they emit pheromones, which attracts other ants."

Ryan reached down and touched the jagged jawbone of one of the mandibles. "These things must really be strong. I saw the way it picked up that goat."

"A normal ant can carry twenty times its own weight," Frank said.

"Are you serious?" Ryan said. "Heck, this thing must weigh..."

"Let me make a rough guesstimate," Dr. Tomie said, "and say maybe three hundred pounds."

"So, you're saying..." Ryan did a quick calculation in his head. "This thing could carry six thousand pounds?"

"Hard to believe, but true," Frank said. "I think we are looking at a new order of insect."

"What do you mean?" Ryan asked.

"Well, about one hundred eighty million years ago, it was believed that South America and Africa were one continent. Over time, they were separated by ocean due to a seismic rift. Once that happened, similar species that were once in parts of the Old World in Africa had to learn to adapt to the New World in South America. Ants are a classic example. You hear more about fire ants and bullets ants in South America and driver ants and army ants in Africa even though the species are closely related."

"And how would you categorize this?" Dr. Tomie said, referring to the giant ant lying dead on her examination table.

"There's definitely an evolutionary unbalance here," Frank said. "For all we know, this might very well be the coming of the Next World."

28

By the time Wanda reached the clinic after leaving the dining hall, her shoulder was beginning to act up again. Once Celeste had told them about the strange siege on the village, Ally and Dillon had been excited about rushing over to see the giant ant. That was until they arrived and saw Frank had rendered the thing almost unrecognizable having dismembered the limbs and dissecting the head and body.

Frank used the tip of a scalpel to illustrate the different organs in the cross-sectioned head. "Because the ant has to break down its food into a liquid before swallowing, the head is made up of various saliva glands that aid with the process." He began pointing and identifying each gland. "This is the labial, over here the pharyngeal gland. You'll notice how it branches off and connects to the brain."

"Where's the heart?" Ryan asked.

"Ants don't have hearts as we know it." Frank moved to a section of the thorax that was cut open on the table. "See this tube?"

Ryan leaned in close. "Yeah, that's it?"

"Runs the entire length of its body, same with the nervous system. If you would..." Frank stopped when he realized Wanda, Ally, and Dillon had been watching him lecture.

"Hi, dear. Feeling any better?"

Wanda took one look at the jumbled ant parts. "Not as bad as that thing."

"Holy moly, Mom. Will you look at that?" Dillon said, running up to the examination table.

"Don't touch," Wanda warned.

Dillon grabbed a severed leg and almost fell backward when the appendage slipped from the table. Ryan reached over and saved his little brother. "Better listen to Mom," he said and positioned the leg where it wouldn't fall off.

Ally walked over and joined Dr. Tomie and Dayo. "I didn't know ants got this huge. Is this an African thing?"

"No, no. This is quite unusual," Dr. Tomie replied.

"So what do you think caused it to get so big?" Dayo asked.

"I think I might know," Celeste said, entering the room. She was carrying a yellow apparatus by the handle that was no bigger than a lunchbox. It had a black push button on the top and a selector dial in the middle next to a round meter.

"You brought a Geiger counter?" Frank asked incredulously. "What in heavens for?"

"You'll see." Celeste walked over to the examining table and turned on the Geiger counter. The reader began to emit a ticking sound. She held up the machine and placed it near the ruined ant parts. The ticking sped up a notch.

"Are we saying this thing is radioactive?" Wanda said. "Ryan, pull your brother away."

Ryan grabbed Dillon and they both stepped back.

Even Dr. Tomie backed away and instructed Ally and Dayo to do the same.

"Frank, step away from that thing," Wanda pleaded with her husband.

"I don't think there's much need for alarm," Celeste said, studying the meter for a moment then turning it off before looking up at everyone. "There's only a residual amount showing on the meter."

"And what does that mean?" Wanda asked.

"Even if this creature was exposed to a high dosage of cosmic radiation, it doesn't seem to be registering high at the moment. I don't know if you're aware, but we're exposed to radiation from the sun every day. The higher the elevation at which a person lives, the more radiation they can expect to receive—something people should consider if they live on the coast and are contemplating moving to the mountains."

"We live in the mountains," Wanda said.

"You mentioned cosmic radiation," Frank interceded. "Why?"

"Well, I believe the meteor showers we have been experiencing might have a direct correlation to the appearance of these abnormal creatures," Celeste responded.

"This isn't the first time we've seen them," Wanda said. She looked over at Frank. "I'll let Frank explain."

Frank faced the group. "A year ago, we went and vacationed at a jungle resort in the Amazon."

"Let's just say it didn't turn out quite like we'd planned. Sort of like this one," Wanda said, directing everyone's attention to her arm in the sling.

"Which is true," Frank had to admit. "Anyway, everything kind of went to hell in a hand basket, and we ended up deep in the jungle in unexplored territory. It was there we saw creatures such as this one." He looked over at Dr. Tomie and saw the skeptical look on her face.

"Mom, you never told us about that," Ally said.

"Yeah, I don't remember any giant ants," Dillon blurted.

"That's because we didn't want you to know. I mean, it all sounds pretty crazy, right? Imagine telling your friends and what they'd think," Wanda said. "Ryan knew, but he promised never to breathe a word of it."

Ryan nodded and gave his sister a sheepish grin.

"But that makes perfect sense," Celeste piped in.

"It does?" Frank said.

"I've been tracking and recording these meteor showers for the past three years."

"So?"

"The first two years, the brief events were over the same remote region of the Amazon. But this year, the meteor activity seems to be directed over the Tomie Reserve."

"Any reason for the change?" Frank said.

"I can't say for sure," Celeste said. "We need to find one of those meteorites."

29

Satisfied that he had gathered enough scientific data from the giant ant's autopsy but not wanting to discard the carcass, Frank asked Dr. Tomie if there was somewhere he might store the remains. She offered her walk-in freezer located in the rear of the kitchen.

After Frank and Ryan had bagged up the cross-sectioned ant and put everything on a pushcart, Wanda, Dillon, and Celeste followed them out of the examination room.

Ally and Dayo got to work cleaning up the mess left by the cross section. They wore masks and rubber gloves and filled two large buckets with soapy water.

Dayo gathered up the goopy protective sheet from the gurney and placed it inside a garbage bag. She went over and began sponging the table, while Ally got down on her hands and knees and scrubbed the tiles clean of the thick gunk that was already starting to dry, making it difficult to clean.

Dr. Tomie had taken the surgical instruments over to the sink and was soaking them in a disinfectant. She carefully took out a set of forceps, put it on a tray to air dry, and turned around. "You know, I'm rather worried."

"About what, Dr. Tomie?" Dayo asked, wringing her sponge out in the bucket.

"Sasha and her cub. What if there are more of these... for lack of a better word, *mutations* out there?"

"But won't they be safe as long as they stay with the pride?" Ally asked. She tossed her grungy sponge into the bucket of water.

"I want to go check on them."

Dayo looked at the clock on the wall. "It will be dark in three hours."

"There's time," Dr. Tomie said. "Hurry, finish up. We'll leave right away."

Fifteen minutes later, Dr. Tomie was behind the wheel of the safari Jeep. Dayo sat up front and Ally occupied the first bench seat.

Ally had to hold on tight as the veterinarian sped across the savanna, the suspension creaking as the vehicle bounced in and out of chuckholes and veered through treacherous ruts, the experience similar to being tossed about in a thrill ride simulator at Universal Studios. At one point, Ally thought for sure Dr. Tomie was going to run them off an escarpment. The doctor cranked the wheel just in the nick of time—a rear tire actually slipping off the edge—narrowly avoiding ending up in a gulch.

They'd been racing across the uneven plain for almost forty-five minutes when Dr. Tomie suddenly put on the brakes. The rear of the safari Jeep shuddered as the vehicle came to a skidding halt.

"I was afraid of this," Dr. Tomie said.

They had stopped just short of the boulder area near the trees where Ally had last seen Sasha and her cub rejoin the pride.

Two male lions were lying on the ground, trampled to death. The rest of the pride was nowhere in sight.

"My God, what happened?" Ally said.

Dayo pointed to the trees.

A large herd of Cape buffalo was standing under the shade.

Ally counted roughly twenty. Each animal was as big as a bull and had to weigh a ton apiece. They had large horns with curled tips that sat across their foreheads like matador hats. Another herd of about the same number was a hundred yards off, except there were a dozen or so calves mingled in the center of the group.

"Black death," Dr. Tomie said.

"What?" Ally asked.

"That is what they call the Cape buffalo," Dayo said.

"Some say they have killed more big game hunters than any other animal on this continent," Dr. Tomie said. "I suppose for that, they should be rewarded."

"I don't understand. You mean the buffalo killed those lions?"

"They are mortal enemies," Dayo said.

"Buffalo will purposely seek out lion cubs and kill them."

"Because they will grow up to be predators, I remember you saying that," Ally said.

"Dr. Tomie, look!"

The buffalo were staring at the Jeep. One by one they began to leave the shade and march out into the sunlight, their heavy hooves kicking up dust. The lead buffalo lowered its head, snorted loudly, and charged.

"Brace yourselves!" Dr. Tomie yelled to Dayo and Ally.

Ally watched in horror as the herd stampeded toward the Jeep.

30

Wanda walked over to Isoba, who was guarding the animal enclosure being used as Duna's jailhouse. Adanna held a garden hose through the bars. Duna was guzzling water greedily from the nozzle.

"That's enough," she said and yanked the hose out.

"Any luck reaching the rangers?" Wanda asked.

"No," Isoba said disappointedly. "I have tried twice but no one answers the radio."

"You haven't seen Ally by chance?"

"She and Dayo left with Dr. Tomie in the safari Jeep more than an hour ago."

"Did they say where they were going?"

"No."

Wanda heard an animal cry and followed the sound to one of the pens. It was Lucy. The baby rhino looked so sad and lonely.

"I bet you're hungry," Wanda said. "You just hold on and I'll be right back."

Wanda cut across the compound and went in the doorway that led into the dining hall and the kitchen. She found a large baby bottle used for the animals. After a brief search in the refrigerator, she found a large jug labeled as Lucy's special formula mix. It took some doing, but she managed to fill the bottle using only one hand.

As she was coming out of the kitchen, Frank and Dillon strolled in.

"Oh, there you are," Frank said. "What's up?"

"Ally's not around and its time for Lucy's feeding."

"Can I do it?" Dillon asked.

"Sure you can." Wanda handed the bottle to her son. He carried it in both hands and hurried off.

"We better keep an eye on him," Wanda said.

They rushed after Dillon. When they caught up to the boy, he was already in Lucy's pen and was holding the bottle up so the rhino could suck the nipple. The white formula was dripping down Lucy's chest and onto her short, thick legs and Dillon's sneakers.

"I think we might have a Kodak moment here," Frank said. He took a small digital camera out of his pocket and took a picture of the boy feeding the baby rhino.

"Let me see."

Frank showed Wanda the new photo on the tiny screen.

"I'd say that's a step up from the petting zoo, wouldn't you say?" Frank turned off his camera and put it back in his pocket.

"I'm a little worried," Wanda said.

"About what?"

"The poacher, Duna. You don't think his brother will really come looking for him?"

"I don't know," Frank said. "Have you spoken with Isoba?"

"He's been trying to reach the rangers, but so far, no luck. Does Dr. Tomie have any guns?"

"I would imagine so. Let's wait until Dillon's finished and we can go ask her."

"She's not here. She left in the big Jeep with Ally and Dayo."

"They did?"

"Do you think they're okay out there?"

"Sure. Gayle wouldn't let anything happen to them."

31

All three women screamed when the safari Jeep was lifted off the ground by the massive bovines and the heavy vehicle flipped upside down. The windshield smashed on the ground and shattered. Dr. Tomie and Dayo were pinned under the seats. The two other bench seats behind Ally had been higher than the one where she sat and saved her from being crushed.

Even though they were trapped and surrounded by the fierce buffalo, there was one factor in their favor. The overturned Jeep had rested on top of a shallow gully that once had been a streambed but was now dried up.

"Are you girls okay?" Dr. Tomie asked, her voice etched with pain.

"Yes, I'm all right," Ally replied, lying a few inches under the bench seat. She was definitely shaken up and bruised but nothing serious.

"Dayo?" Dr. Tomie reached over and shook the woman's shoulder. Dayo let out a groan.

"How are you, Dr. Tomie?" Ally asked. "Are you hurt?"

"My right foot is wedged under something."

"Let me try and help." Ally squeezed out from under the back and crawled in the depression until she reached the doctor. She grabbed Dr. Tomie by the shoulders and tried to pull her free.

"No, please...stop. It's my ankle."

Ally could hear the heavy stamping of the buffalos as their thick bodies kept brushing up against the Jeep's bumpers and fenders. She glanced over and saw Dayo open her eyes.

"Dayo!"

"My arm..."

Ally could see the splintered bone sticking out the skin of Dayo's arm.

Dr. Tomie had also seen Dayo's severe injury. "You must straighten out her arm. Then tie it with a splint."

"I don't think..."

"It is all right, Ally," Dayo said, groggily. "You can do it."

"Ally, it must be done," Dr. Tomie said.

Rather than waste time self-doubting herself, Ally found an old t-shirt that had been left in the Jeep and began tearing it into long strips. She found a piece of broken door panel and bent it in half to use as a splint. Scooting around on her side, Ally pressed the toe of her boot into Dayo's armpit and grabbed the woman's wrist with both hands. "Are you ready?"

"Yes," Dayo said bravely.

"On the count of three," Ally said. "One..." Ally yanked as hard as she could.

Dayo screamed, the noise so loud that it startled the buffalos and even caused some of them to back away from the Jeep, and then she passed out.

"She's out cold," Dr. Tomie said. "Fix her up before she wakes up."

Ally inspected the fracture, praying that she had properly aligned the bone. She hated the thought of Dayo never gaining full control of the arm and that she would be to blame. She put the crumpled door panel around the break and fastened the splint tight with the torn strips. Once she was done, she let out a sigh of relief.

"Nice work, Ally," Dr. Tomie said.

"What about you?"

"I'm afraid there isn't much you can do. We're just going to have to wait until help arrives."

"But no one knows where we are." Ally gazed out from under the Jeep, hoping for a way to sneak out, but all she could see were the many hooves of the buffalo as they milled around the Jeep.

Then something caught her eye…

Just beyond the herd, a white speck in the grass.

It was Sasha's cub.

32

"I think we need to go look for them," Wanda said, finishing her coffee and setting her cup on the drain board. "It'll be dark soon."

"Agreed," Frank said. "But you're in no shape to go." He placed his empty mug in the kitchen sink.

"I know. We better go talk with Isoba. He must have some idea where they might have gone."

They left the kitchen and went out through the rear of the building. As they crossed the compound, they saw Ryan and Celeste standing inside Lucy's pen, helping Dillon care for the baby rhino.

Frank and Wanda gave them a wave and continued on to Duna's improvised jailhouse. Isoba and Adanna were sitting on the ground outside the animal enclosure under a narrow strip of shade, having a late supper of semolina pasta.

Isoba put his bowl down on the dirt when he saw Frank and Wanda approach.

"We're concerned that Dr. Tomie hasn't returned yet," Frank said.

"My husband was wondering if you might help him look for them."

"I have to stay here. With our prisoner," Isoba said.

Duna approached the bars to look out, but when he went to touch the steel, he immediately jerked his hands back. Wanda could only imagine how hot it must be in the adobe enclosure. Even though the man's face and scalp glistened with sweat, he didn't seem distressed by the extreme heat.

It was as though he knew it wouldn't be long before he would be freed.

"Give me a gun and I'll stand watch. I'm sure Adanna could use a break."

"But your arm," Isoba said.

"Don't worry about that," Wanda said. "I still have one good hand."

"Wanda's pretty good with a gun," Frank said. "I've seen her in action."

"All right. I, too, am worried about Dr. Tomie and the others," Isoba finally admitted. "I think I know where they may have gone."

"Thank you, Isoba," Wanda said.

"First, let me get you that gun," Isoba said, then turned to his daughter. "If he gives you any trouble—"

"Shoot him?" Adanna said eagerly.

"No! Ignore him!"

Adanna gave her father a sheepish grin that said she was only kidding. But there was a dark look in her eyes that spoke differently.

Frank and Wanda followed Isoba inside the building. He took them down the main corridor then turned down a hallway. He stopped at a door, took a ring of keys out of his trouser pocket, found the correct key, and unlocked the door. He pushed open the door and they stepped into a small room partitioned in half by a wire mesh fence stretching from the floor to the ceiling.

Isoba unlocked the gate and stepped inside the caged area. Frank and Wanda joined him in the modest gunroom. Ten shotguns stood upright on their stocks in one gun cabinet. Seven hunting rifles hung horizontally on the wall. A large red metal cabinet that a mechanic might stow hand tools took up one end of the cage.

Isoba went over and opened the top drawer. It was sectioned in three parts. Each one contained a revolver and half a dozen boxes of ammunition.

He opened the next drawer. It contained semi-automatic pistols with full clips already loaded with bullets. "There are more guns in the other drawers."

"This should do fine," Wanda said. She picked a nine-millimeter Beretta and placed three clips inside her sling.

"Looks like you're set," Frank said.

"Now go find Ally."

33

"I see Sasha's cub," Ally said excitedly.

"Where?" Dr. Tomie asked, straining her neck to look out from under the Jeep.

"It's hiding in the short grass just by that grove of trees. Can you see it?"

"No, but I'll take your word for it. I wonder where Sasha is? It's not like her to abandon her cub."

"I don't see her," Ally said. She turned to the doctor. "Should I go get it?"

"It would be too dangerous," Dayo said, having just come to after passing out when Ally set her broken arm. "The buffalo would kill you."

"I can outrun them."

"Don't be silly, you're not going," Dr. Tomie said.

"But I could grab the cub and be back before you know it."

"Absolutely not."

Ally stuck her head out to get a better look at the terrain. She ducked back suddenly when a buffalo stepped up to the side of the Jeep and stomped the ground.

"What if you were to distract them?"

"No, you're not going."

"Does the horn work?"

Dr. Tomie glanced at the pad in the center of the steering wheel.

Ally reached over and pressed down on the pad, blasting the horn.

Some of the buffalo backed off, frightened by the sound.

"See how they moved away," Ally said.

"I can't let you do this," Dr. Tomie protested.

"If the buffalo see the cub, they'll kill it. You said so yourself. Let me do this. Once I grab the cub, I can hide in those trees. The buffalo won't be able to get to me. I can wait there until help comes."

"Frank and Wanda would be very upset with me if they knew I let you do this."

"On the contrary, they would be proud. You know how they are."

"It's almost dark." Dr. Tomie reached over to the glove compartment and popped it open. She reached inside and handed Ally a small flashlight. "Here, you might need this."

"Okay," Ally said. She realized the doctor had resigned to the fact that if she didn't let Ally go save the cub, it would only be a matter of time before the whelp became hungry and began crying, drawing the buffalo to its hiding place.

"Let me know when you're ready," Dr. Tomie said, placing her hand above the horn pad in the center of the steering wheel.

Ally got flat on her stomach and looked out. She saw thick, black legs and the buffalos' mighty hooves, pawing at the ground and kicking up dust. She could also see the white cub hunkered down in the grass.

"Now!" she yelled.

Dr. Tomie pressed down the pad and the horn blared.

Ally crawled out from under the Jeep and scrambled to her feet. A few of the buffalo had trotted away, leaving a small gap in the herd. She took advantage of the situation and ran between two bulls. She slapped one on the rump and the animal spun around. Ally ducked between the massive heads as they butted horns. The larger buffalo slammed into the other bull and sent it reeling back a few feet.

Ally snuck a glance over her shoulder and saw the big bull charge after her. She ran has hard as she could, lengthening her stride, pouring it on like she did every time when she was in high school, racing down the track for the finish line. Only this time it wasn't for a ribbon or medal—it was to save an innocent creature from certain doom. Not to mention her own.

When the cub saw Ally running toward it, the cat let out an "Eeeyap" and bared its teeth. Ally stopped long enough to snatch the cub up by the scruff and tucked it under her arm, pinning the legs so that she wouldn't be scratched. She could hear the thundering hooves behind her.

Instead of running straight and getting trampled by the buffalo, Ally dodged to the right and headed for the nearest tree, thinking she would be safe. But she soon realized her mistake as the trunks were spaced several feet apart and would not offer any barrier of protection. She kept running, veering in and out of the trees to throw off the buffalo, but it was relentless and continued the pursuit.

It was difficult making out the contour of the ground in the dark. If there were a rock or an exposed root in her path, she might trip.

The cub yelped and squirmed, but Ally held it tight like a linebacker clutching a football.

She kept running and had no idea how far she'd gone or where she was. When she could run no more, she stopped and leaned up against the backside of a tree trunk to catch her breath. She took a moment to listen but heard nothing except a few birdcalls up in the overhead branches.

Ally thought if she yelled, Dr. Tomie and Dayo might hear her and honk the horn, give her a direction in which she could return. But that would mean facing the buffalos again.

She had to find a place to hold up until help came. She took the flashlight from her pocket and turned it on. The beam shone on the cub's face. The amber-colored eyes twinkled in the light. The cub glared at Ally and hissed.

"Easy there, little one. Just cool your jets. Don't forget I just saved your life."

The cub looked at Ally, still not sure of what to make of her.

"Don't worry, I won't bite you."

Ally watched as the cub's upper lip curled and it showed off its tiny fangs. "And I expect you to give me the same courtesy."

34

As Isoba gunned the Jeep transport across the savanna, the bright high beams paved the way through the pitch dark. The halogen lights on the cab roof disrupted many animals on their nocturnal hunts. Some froze in their tracks, others bolted into the bleak night.

Frank could feel the panting breath of the Anatolian shepherd on his neck as Samson tried to stay planted on the rear seat but was bounced about in the cab.

"There they are," Isoba said. "I was right. Dr. Tomie came to check on Sasha,"

"Jesus, what happened," Frank said when he saw the safari Jeep flipped over in a ditch. He counted a dozen or more Cape buffalos surrounding the wrecked vehicle.

Isoba stopped the truck. He reached back and opened the door for Samson, then got out his door. He reached in and grabbed his rifle. Frank climbed out his side.

"Be careful," Isoba warned.

Frank leaned in the cab and grabbed a hunting rifle he had brought along. He pulled back the bolt and rammed a cartridge into the breech.

"Dr. Tomie!" Isoba called out. "Can you hear me?"

"Yes," the doctor hollered back. "We're trapped under the Jeep. Dayo's arm is broken, and I'm pinned down."

Frank looked at Isoba. "What about Ally?"

Isoba gave him a shrug then yelled, "Hold on! We will get you out!"

"What about the buffalos?" Frank said.

Isoba shouted to Samson. The dog began barking and charged the buffalos. Some of the bovines retreated and scattered into the low shrub. A few decided to hold their ground.

Isoba fired his rifle in the air.

The remaining buffalos turned tail and trotted into the darkness. Samson took off after them and disappeared in the night but quickly returned, chest puffed out and wagging his tail.

With the buffalos now out of the way, Frank and Isoba ran over to the upside down vehicle. Frank stood and held the flashlight while Isoba got down on his hands and knees and peered underneath the overturned Jeep.

"I don't think we can get out," Dr. Tomie said. "You're going to have to figure a way to lift the Jeep."

Isoba stood and turned to Frank. "I'll need help with the winch."

"All right." Frank stood by while Isoba got back in the cab and maneuvered the front bumper of the truck over to the side of the Jeep.

Frank leaned his rifle against the bumper. He grabbed the hook and began pulling out the cable wound around the winch. He strung the cable over the chassis and anchored the hook on the side of the Jeep.

"Okay, nice and slow," he yelled over to Isoba.

Isoba activated the winch. The cable became taut and started to wind back onto the spool.

Frank could hear creaking metal as the Jeep rose a couple feet. "Okay, stop!" He got down and looked under the vehicle. "Dr. Tomie, do you have enough room to free yourself?"

"Yes. I think we can crawl out, but you will have to help us."

Frank reached in and grabbed Dr. Tomie by the arms and pulled her slowly out from under the vehicle. He went back under and was able to help Dayo out as well but then he was surprised Ally wasn't there.

"Where's Ally?"

"She went to save Sasha's cub," Dayo said. "Back in those trees."

"What? You mean to tell me you sent her out there?"

"No, Frank. She insisted on going. I'm sorry. I know it was wrong."

"We have to get Dr. Tomie and Dayo back to the clinic," Isoba said, rushing over from the truck.

"Wait a minute, we can't just leave Ally out there." Frank cupped his hands around his mouth and yelled Ally's name over and over again but there was no answer.

He kept shouting, even when his voice became hoarse.

"Please," Isoba said, "I need your help."

Frank assisted Isoba and they carried the doctor to the rear of the truck and made her as comfortable as possible in the flatbed. Isoba helped his daughter up to sit with Dr. Tomie.

"I have to go find Ally," Frank said.

"It will be too dangerous in the dark," Isoba said. "Especially on foot."

"I don't care. I have to find her."

"We will come back, when it is light. It will be easier to pick up her tracks."

Frank could hear Dr. Tomie groaning in the back of the truck. He wanted to argue the point, convince Isoba to help him go find Ally, but he knew it was futile. Dr. Tomie and Dayo were in great pain and need of medical attention.

He cupped his hands around his mouth and yelled one last time, "Ally!"

This time he did get an answer. The distant roar of a lion followed by a cackling hyena.

He didn't know which he dreaded worse.

Having to leave Ally out here all by herself...

Or going back and telling Wanda of his decision.

35

Even though Ally tried her best to subdue the fidgety cub, it still managed to free a back paw and scratch her arm. Her little rescue mission hadn't gone quite like she'd planned. She feared if she put the cub on the ground, it would scamper off, and she would be forced to chase after it.

There was no telling what was lurking out there in the dark—waiting hungrily for something to come its way.

So when she shined the flashlight on the entrance to a small cave, she was relieved. It looked like a good spot to hold up for the night. Once inside, she could finally put the cub down and rest her arm, get the small creature situated where she could guard and prevent it from escaping.

Bending down, Ally shined the light inside the cave. The tunnel was about four feet high and went back approximately twenty feet. She couldn't tell if it stopped at a dead end or if there was an elbow leading to another passageway.

"Come on, you," Ally said, gazing into the cub's face. "We're sleeping here for the night." She had to stoop as she entered the cave. She didn't want to venture too far back. There was a strange but familiar odor inside the cave that she couldn't quite put her finger on.

She sat down on the hard ground. Keeping one arm around the cub, Ally reached down and unbuckled her belt. After she drew the belt out of her pant loops, she slipped the belt through the buckle and formed a noose. She slipped the noose over the cub's small head, and cinched it tight enough the baby lion couldn't pull its head out, but loose enough so as not to choke it.

The cub immediately fought the restraint.

"Now, now, little one. Relax. No one's going to hurt you."

The cub continued to tug and hissed at his captor.

"Sooner or later, you're going to realize that I'm doing this for your own good."

It took about two minutes of yanking and squirming before the cub came to the conclusion that no matter how hard it fought to get free, it was wasting its time. The cub stopped struggling, and lay on its belly with its chin on its front paws.

"Good boy. See, that wasn't so hard."

Ally sat back against the rock wall and tried to make herself as comfortable as possible. The cub inched over and nestled up against her hip. Ally reached down and stroked its fur. It wasn't long before the content cub began purring.

"Don't worry, little one. We'll find your mother."

36

Wanda was fit to be tied when Frank told her that Ally was still out there somewhere on the savanna. She was so upset that she had even slammed her hand down on a table in the hall, which only shot a jolt of pain through her injured collarbone.

"Damn it, Frank, how could you just leave her out there?"

"Do you think I wanted to? Hell, no," Frank said, wanting nothing better than to punch something himself. "But Isoba insisted we come back. He said it would be impossible to find her in the dark on foot. That we should wait until daybreak. I felt I had no choice. Besides, there were Dr. Tomie and Dayo to consider. They were in a lot of pain. I'm sorry."

Wanda glared at Frank.

"Okay, you're right. I shouldn't have left her. Please, let's not fight."

Wanda turned away for a moment then looked back at Frank. "Promise you'll find her."

"I will, I swear."

"I don't want to fight either."

They'd taken a moment to go off into another part of the building to quarrel, leaving Dr. Tomie and Dayo in the examination room.

"We should get back, see if there's anymore we can do to help out."

Frank and Wanda went back down the corridor and joined the others.

Dr. Tomie was wrapping wet plaster strips around Dayo's left forearm that would later dry into a cast. She was sitting on a swivel stool with her right foot propped up on top of one of the casters. A thick bandage was wrapped around her ankle.

"I took an x-ray. Ally did a great job setting Dayo's arm," Dr. Tomie said.

"How's your ankle?" Frank asked.

"Swollen, but I don't think it's broken." Dr. Tomie looked at Wanda. "Would it make you feel any better if I told you Isoba made the right decision?"

"No."

"I didn't think so. If I hadn't been so worried about Sasha this never would have happened."

"That's part of your job. Being a vet. I know how it is. Duty and all," Wanda said.

Frank came up and put his arm around Wanda. "Don't worry, we'll—"

"Hey, you guys!" Ryan yelled, storming into the room. "It's happening again. Hurry!"

Frank and Wanda rushed out of the room and followed Ryan down the corridor.

They raced outside and ran over to the deck that overlooked the savanna. Celeste and Dillon were gazing up at the stars.

"Over there!" Celeste shouted, pointing at the night sky.

A green streak shot across the black backdrop dotted with white pinpricks of light. Another meteor came down in the north; then another one not too far away.

They continued to watch. Dillon got excited each time he saw a meteor. This time the event lasted slightly longer than the previous night.

"How many was that, Celeste?" Frank asked.

"Thirty-six."

"That's more than last night."

"That's right."

"You mean that's it?" Dillon said.

"Guess so," Celeste said.

"Bummer."

"Well, that sure was something," Ryan said, turning to his mother. "Right, Mom?"

But Wanda's thoughts were a million miles away.

"Mom, are you okay?"

Wanda turned and said, "Yes, I'm fine."

Ryan looked around. "Where's Ally?"

Wanda and Frank exchanged glances.

"We didn't want you to worry," Frank said.

"Worry? About what?"

"Ally's missing."

37

Ally woke up when she heard the noise. She shined the flashlight deep inside the cave. At first, she wasn't sure what she was seeing. It looked like a hundred thin stalks of wheat twitching in a breeze though there was no airflow moving through the stagnant cave.

She scooted onto her knees to get a better look and accidentally bumped the lion cub, waking it up. That's when she heard a multitude of skittering feet.

A horde of long-antennae crickets—each the size of a large man's shoe—raced towards her. She never knew crickets could get so big. There were so many they had to climb over one another in order to squeeze down the narrow tunnel. They covered the walls and the floor.

Ally went to grab the cub, but it was already going for the crickets and pulled the belt from her hand. "Hey, get back here!"

The cub pounced on a few of the crickets, snapping their spindly legs. Then the large insects swarmed the cub, so many that Ally couldn't see the young lion.

Ally, too, had to fend off the bothersome bugs. She had handled crickets as a child and never remembered ever being bitten by one. But these crickets were different—they were bigger and had sizable jaws that pinched her flesh like tiny pliers.

She could hear the lion cub yelp under the blanket of crickets.

"It's check-out time," Ally said. She leaned over and shoved her hand into the mound of crickets until she felt fur. She pulled the lion cub out of the turmoil and brushed off the crickets still clinging to the hissing cat.

She ducked her head and rushed out of the cave. She ran a few steps before stopping to look back. The crickets hadn't followed her out. They had no intention of coming out of the cave and had only been trying to scare her away.

"That wasn't very hospitable," Ally said.

She was surprised to see the morning sun creeping up on the horizon, realizing that she and the cub had slept soundly in the cave. She turned off her flashlight and stuffed it in her back pocket. Now that it was light, she might have a chance of finding her way back to the Jeep and wait with Dr. Tomie and Dayo until help came. Hopefully the buffalos had grown bored and moved on.

Ally put the cub down. As soon as its paws were on the ground, the cub tried to bolt.

"You're not going anywhere," she said and tugged on the belt.

The cub halted and swung around to bite the leather. Thinking she might be able to lead the cub like a dog, Ally started walking, but the cub would have none of it. It twirled around, ending up on its back, and shook its head to get out of the strap.

"I guess this isn't going to work." Ally bent down and picked the cub up. She was expecting a fight, but instead the cub calmed down right away. "Well, now, aren't we the smart one. Why walk when you can get a free ride."

Ally turned in a circle, hoping to recall anything that might give her a clue as to which way she should go. Nothing looked familiar.

So she headed in the direction of the sunrise.

38

Ryan woke to a pounding on the door. He opened his eyes, glanced out the window and saw that it was light outside. He climbed out of bed, went over, and opened the door a crack to look out. Celeste peered back at him.

"Ryan, I have the keys to the Jeep."

"Yeah?"

"We can go look for your sister."

"I was hoping to go with Frank and Isoba."

"They've already gone," Celeste said, pushing open the door and stepping inside the cottage.

"When did they leave?"

"About half an hour ago. You coming or what?"

"Yeah, but what about my little brother?" Ryan looked over at Dillon, who was still fast asleep.

"Leave him a note," Celeste said. She went over to the nightstand and opened the drawer. She took out a small notepad and pen and handed them to Ryan.

"Let me get dressed first." Standing in only his boxers, Ryan grabbed a t-shirt and a pair of loose-fitting trousers off the end of the bed. He put them on then slipped on his socks and boots.

He took the pen and pad from Celeste and scribbled a short note. He tore off the slip of paper and set it on the nightstand by Dillon's bed.

"Come on, before he wakes up," Celeste said, standing in the doorway.

Ryan walked across the room and gently closed the door. But when the latch clicked, the noise stirred Dillon in his sleep and he rolled over. The edge of his pillow brushed the note off the nightstand. The slip of paper floated down and fell under the bed.

Outside, Ryan and Celeste ran across the yard to where the Willys Jeep was parked. Celeste handed Ryan the ignition key and they got into the old military four-wheeler.

"Did you see which way they went?" Ryan asked.

"Just follow that compass on the dashboard and go west."

Ryan started the engine. Before he put it into gear, he looked down and noticed the Geiger counter down by Celeste's feet, along with her computer bag. "Why are you bringing those?"

"Thought as long as we're looking for your sister, we might get lucky and come across one of those meteorites."

"Right now, all I care about is finding Ally."

"I understand."

"Okay then. You said west."

"That's right."

Ryan looked at the compass, then turned the Jeep around.

He tromped on the accelerator and headed due west.

39

Isoba drove toward the rising sun while Frank gazed through a pair of binoculars in hopes of spotting Ally wandering the plain. Even Samson was on high alert, sitting in the back seat and staring out the side window.

"Is that Gatura's village up ahead?" Frank asked when he saw the structures.

"Yes," Isoba answered.

"Where is everyone?"

"Let's stop for a minute."

Frank continued to scan the binoculars, searching for any sign of life. There was none—no goats, sheep, or chickens. "I wonder if the ants came back and they had to abandon the village."

Isoba pulled up to the side of one of the dwellings and shut off the engine. He got out of the truck, grabbed his rifle, and opened the door for Samson to jump out.

Frank climbed out on his side and brought his rifle.

"This is very strange," Isoba said, looking around.

It was deathly quiet. No sound, not even a cicada.

"We better get going," Frank said, anxious to get back in the truck and continue the search for Ally.

"Not until we look through the village," Isoba said.

Frank was getting irritated but held back from snapping at Isoba. He knew the man was only concerned about the villagers. Even though it was just after six in the morning, it was already unbearably hot. Whatever could cause the people to leave the sanctuary of their homes and expose themselves to this torrid heat?

Isoba gave Samson a hand signal and the dog darted off between the huts.

Frank walked over to a dwelling and peeked inside the open doorway. The interior was circular in design. A long shelf protruding from the dried mud ran completely around the room, filled with hand-painted plates and weaved baskets. Different patterned rugs covered most of the dirt floor. Against the wall were a variety of mismatched chairs that looked like they had been collected throughout the years.

But there was no one inside.

He went to the next hut. The same.

Frank was about to search the next dwelling when suddenly Samson began to bark and Isoba yelled, "Frank! Over here!"

Judging by the urgency of his voice, Frank knew Isoba had discovered something alarming.

Frank had no idea what to expect when he ran over—certainly not an emperor scorpion the size of a Chevy Suburban with pinchers big enough to pick up fifty-five gallon drums.

Isoba was trying his best to hold back his dog, but Samson was eager for a fight, even though the odds were in favor of the giant arthropod. The scorpion's exoskeleton was a shiny black, and it stood as tall as Isoba. It took a step forward, spreading its enormous pinchers then snapping them shut with loud *clacks*. Its eight legs sidestepped in unison to the left as it raised its curved tail high, positioning the stinger.

Frank aimed and fired his rifle.

The bullet creased the top of the scorpion's head.

He'd been trying for its eyes—the thing had eight black orbs for crying out loud—figuring it was a sure shot and he couldn't possibly miss, but he had.

Ejecting the spent shell, Frank closed the bolt and shot again. This time the bullet struck the right pedipalp, disabling the pincher at the elbow. The wounded arthropod stumbled back.

Isoba kept a tight grip on Samson's collar and pulled the dog through the doorway into a hut.

The scorpion lunged, extending its left pincher inside the opening, but it was too wide to fit completely through.

Frank heard the loud *clacking* of the giant pincher as the arachnid tried to grab Isoba and Samson. He moved in and pointed the muzzle of his rifle directly at the center of the scorpion's face and fired. This time he did hit one of the eyes, which erupted in a dark gooey mist as the bullet slammed through the scorpion's head and scrambled its nervous system. As the black abomination fell, it impaled itself with its own stinger.

Why it did that, Frank couldn't say. Perhaps it was a reflex—certainly not a feeble suicide attempt. Emperor scorpions were immune to their own venom.

"It's safe to come out."

Isoba stuck his head out and saw the massive scorpion, dead on the ground. He let go of Samson. The dog rushed over, sniffed, and paced around the creature.

Frank looked at Isoba. "I guess now we know what caused the villagers to leave."

40

With the lion cub under her arm, Ally hiked up a grassy knoll and stopped when she reached the crest. She gazed down the slope and saw what was once a watering hole but was now a mud pit due to lack of rain. The only visible sign of freeflowing water was a small creek thirty yards away that ran along the base of a rise but no longer fed into the depression.

As she started down the hill, she noticed something moving around in the center of the mud pit.

"Oh my God," Ally said when she realized it was Sasha. The lioness was covered in mud, her white head the only part of her not smirched. She was wallowing up to her chest. Each time she struggled to get free, the soggy bottom sucked her back down.

Ally saw a Cape buffalo, also trapped in the muck. By the way the animal was positioned, the buffalo must have been chasing Sasha and the two of them ended up getting stuck.

The buffalo was only ten feet into the mud, but Sasha was twice as far and surely doomed. The bovine's belly was still above the surface, and it was making a concerted effort, pulling each hoof out of the boggy ground and stepping back toward the solid bank.

Sasha saw Ally, and the big cat roared.

Ally put the cub down on the ground. "Stay put."

But of course it didn't listen and scampered toward the edge of the mud pit to be with its mother. Ally scurried after and scooped up the impetuous cub.

Ally glanced around and saw a large rock that had to weigh at least thirty pounds. She brought the cub over, strung out the belt being used as a leash and put her foot on the end. She picked up the heavy rock and placed it on the length of the belt, anchoring the cub so that it couldn't run off. The cub tried to pull away but got nowhere.

Sasha was growing tired, thrashing in the mud. Soon the damp earth would be hard as cement from the baking sun.

The buffalo had gotten free. The weary animal stood wobbly, its legs covered with chunky gray mud. Ally was afraid it would see her and charge.

Instead, it just turned and sauntered off into the grassland.

Maybe if she waited long enough, the mud would dry enough for her to walk across and she could figure a way to free Sasha. But it seemed an impossible task. How would she dig the enormous lioness out? For one, she didn't have any tools. And for two, the big cat would no doubt maul her the moment she got within reach.

Ally walked up and down the shoreline trying to think of way to rescue Sasha.

Then a strange buzzing sound caught her ear. It was coming from overhead.

Ally craned her head back and looked up.

Three giant wasps swooped over the mud pit. They had black bodies with yellow legs and were six feet long. Their beating wings seemed invisible as they hovered and collected large mud balls with their feet.

One of the wasps changed direction, thrust out its stinger, and flew toward Sasha.

"Get away from her!" Ally yelled. She looked down, picked up a softball-size rock and heaved it at the menacing wasp.

She put too much oomph into the pitch and overthrew the rock, missing her target. She reached for another stone, but stopped when she heard a truck engine.

A Land Rover pulled up just above the creek. The driver's door swung open and a big man stepped out holding a rifle. He looped the gun strap around his forearm, pressed the gunstock up against the front of his shoulder, and after gazing through a high-powered scope, fired.

Ally turned and saw the wasp that was about to attack Sasha blow apart like a clay pigeon at a skeet shoot. The other two wasps took flight.

"Thank God, you came when you did," Ally hollered up to the man.

Finally, help had arrived.

41

Celeste had been constantly consulting her laptop since they had left the animal compound, and twice, had instructed Ryan to veer off the compass's course. When she told him to change again, he finally put his foot down and brought the Jeep to a skidding halt.

"I thought we were looking for Ally?"

"We are," Celeste replied.

"No, we're not. Tell me the truth. You have no idea which way they went."

"Ryan, I'm telling you the—" and then her voice trailed off when she saw the devastation up ahead. "What in the world?"

Ryan put both hands on the steering wheel and stared at the stand of trees.

"Those are jackalberry trees," Celeste said. "Or what's left of them."

There were over a dozen trees that looked like they had been struck by lightning. Some were reduced to stumps, others split up the middle, all of them with branches snapped off.

Large heaps of sawdust—some as high as two feet—surrounded the base of the mutilated trees.

"These trees are prevalent throughout the savanna woodlands and are a major food source of fruit and leaves for most of the wildlife around here," Celeste said.

Ryan could see scores of purple fruit lying on the ground. "Looks like they've been put through a wood chipper."

"It does. Which is weird."

"Why's that?"

"I did some reading about the area before I came out here," Celeste said. "Apparently, the jackalberry trees have very dense wood. It's so hard it's virtually impervious to termites. Which is odd when you think about it, as these trees thrive in churned soil created by these eusocial insects."

"So what did destroy these trees?"

Celeste stepped out of the Jeep and put her laptop on the seat. "I'd like to take a look around."

"Whoa, what about Ally?" Ryan protested.

"It'll only take a minute."

"Jesus," Ryan said. He turned off the engine and climbed out.

"Let's go this way." Celeste walked along the outskirt of the decimated trees toward a grassy knoll. Ryan caught up to her and noticed she was following a large trail of what appeared to be ground up tan bark.

"What is that?" he asked.

"Fecal pellets."

Ryan didn't say anymore until they had rounded the base of the hillock and gotten to the other side.

"Holy shit!' he swore as he looked up.

"That is one hell of a giant termite mound," Celeste agreed.

The insect-built structure was fifty feet tall and twenty feet in circumference at the base. Clumped dirt tapered up into five separate spires that looked like an outstretched hand with vent holes resembling broken-off fingers.

From where they stood, they could hear activity within the giant mound.

"Do you think it's safe to be here?" Ryan asked.

"Maybe you should be asking him." Celeste pointed to a medium-sized animal with long ears and a tubular pig-like snout routing at the base of the termite mound.

"Is that an aardvark?"

"Certainly is."

"I've never seen one before except in pictures."

"Well, now you have."

Ryan and Celeste watched as the African ant bear used its sharp claws and began digging a hole in the mound. The insectivore was half inside the burrow when it suddenly backed out.

A yellowish-brown, winged termite soldier—the size of the aardvark—scurried out of the hole. Another giant termite followed, then more.

"What the hell?" Ryan yelled.

The aardvark rushed off but not before a winged termite landed on its back and blew up like an M80 firework, killing itself and the animal.

"Jesus, did you see that?" Ryan yelled, but Celeste was already hightailing it back to the Jeep because more termites were exiting the mound and sprouting their wings.

42

When Tyrone Vane drove up on the ridge and looked down, he couldn't believe his luck when he saw the enormous lioness stuck in the mud pit. He turned off the engine and grabbed Gwala's rifle from the passenger seat. Opening his door, he got out, wrapped the sling around his forearm, and looked through the scope.

At first he thought an ordinary wasp had flown onto the lens because it was enormous under the magnification. But then he realized the insect was actually hovering over the lioness—and it was gigantic. He put the thing in the middle of the crosshairs, pulled the trigger, and watched with satisfaction as it burst apart like a ruptured water balloon. He lowered the rifle and saw two more giant wasps fly away, scared off by the loud rifle blast.

This was turning out be one incredible day.

First the baboons with the huge ticks, and now giant wasps!

He got back into the Land Rover, started the engine, and plunged down the embankment. He drove the four-wheel drive vehicle into the creek. Halfway across, the water level reached midway up the doors. Gray smoke belched out the ends of the upright exhaust pipes just above the roof.

Vane goosed the gas pedal and the Land Rover emerged out of the water onto the bank. He threw the shifter into park and switched off the engine.

As he started to get out, a young woman ran up. "Thank God, you're here. I really need your help."

"Help?"

"The lioness. Can you help me get her out?"

"Why would you want to do that?" Vane asked curiously.

"So I can reunite her with her cub." The woman pointed to a white baby lion tethered to a rock.

He figured the exotic lion cub was worth somewhere around $50,000 on the black market, but he wasn't really interested. Once he had his trophy shot, he could care less what happened to the cub.

"Who are you?" he asked.

"I'm Ally. Ally Rafferty. I'm staying at the Tomie Reserve."

Vane didn't like the sound of that. "You're not a ranger, are you?"

"Oh, no. I'm here on vacation with my family."

He looked out at the lioness trapped in the bog, which did propose a problem. Sure, it was an easy shot, but then what? How would he get his picture with his kill? He certainly wasn't going to traipse out there in the mud. He doubted if he could get two steps before the mud sucked his boots off. No, there had to be a better way.

"I think I may know a way to get her out," Ally said.

"Let's hear it." Vane was more than up for any suggestions.

"See that tree over there?" Ally pointed to a tall tree with a narrow trunk. "I bet if we try cutting it down, we can shove it over onto the mud pit. Then we can throw a rope around Sasha and pull her out."

"Just like that." He was surprised to hear her say the lioness's name.

"What, you don't have an axe?"

"Better still, I have a chainsaw."

"Is that a winch on the front of your car?"

"Certainly is."

"So, what are we waiting for?" Ally said.

Vane was used to others doing the work for him and wasn't overly excited about getting sweaty and dirty. He knew how to use the chainsaw and how to operate the winch; and had to admit, the young woman had a well thought out plan.

Seemed a shame he was going to spoil it.

He got to work and dug the chainsaw out from under some gear in the cargo hold.

Cutting down the tree had been easier than he thought. He'd given the trunk a quick shove, praying that the tree didn't fall on top of the lioness. It narrowly missed her by a few feet, which got her to growl and bare her teeth.

"Do you have a rope?" Ally asked. "I can walk across and loop it around Sasha."

"I don't think so."

"What do you mean?"

"That cat will rip your head off. I have a better idea." Vane went back to the rear of the Land Rover and rummaged around until he found a tranquilizer gun. He opened a small box containing sedative darts and inserted one into the chamber. He grabbed a coil of rope and some cargo straps that he could join together and fabricate a harness.

Vane walked around the side of the vehicle and joined Ally.

"Here's how this is going to work. I shoot her with a dart, and when we think she's pretty much out, you go out there and hook this around her," he said and handed her the harness.

Vane hit the lioness on the first shot. He figured it would take a few minutes for the sedative to kick in. He still needed to uncoil the cable on the winch and hook the rope and harness on the end.

"Why don't you sit in the Land Rover, enjoy the A/C," Vane said.

"Okay, thanks. Can I bring the cub?"

"Why don't we leave it where it is for now."

"Sure, okay." Ally glanced over at the cub, and then walked slowly over to the passenger side. She opened the door and got inside.

Vane opened the driver's door and started the vehicle. Cool air blew out from the vents on the dashboard. He engaged the winch and shut the door.

It took him a couple minutes to splay out the cable and fasten the rope and harness. He looked up and saw Ally sitting up front. She was staring down at something.

He walked up and looked through the side window.

Ally was viewing the pictures on his tablet.

43

"Uh-oh," Ryan said as he ran through the ruined timber and saw the sounder of warthogs milling around the Jeep. There were maybe twenty, eating the jackalberry fruit lying on the ground.

The pigs had large tusks and were mostly gray with thick manes running midway down their spines. The males were as big as 300 pounds, the females and younger ones closer to 200 pounds, along with a few piglets, their faces pressed in the purplish mush.

"Oh, God, what'd we do?" Celeste said in a panic.

Ryan glanced over his shoulder and saw the giant termites with their enormous wings flying towards them. He reached down and picked up a broken-off branch to use as a club. Striking one of those monstrous termites was probably a bad idea, especially after he'd seen the one land on the aardvark and blow up like some crazy kamikaze.

"We need a diversion," Ryan said, dropping the branch. "Grab some rocks so we can get the pigs' attention."

"You sure that's a good idea?"

"Got a better one?"

Celeste bent down and picked up a baseball-size rock.

Ryan grabbed a couple stones and heaved one in the air. It came down and struck a boar on the rump. The swine snorted, turned its body half around, and looked straight at Ryan but didn't charge like he had hoped.

Celeste threw her rock and hit another pig on the head. This time she got more of a reaction because the angry animal let out a loud grunt and broke into a fast run, spurring on followers, until the entire group was stampeding toward Ryan and Celeste.

Ryan grabbed Celeste's hand. "Hurry, up that tree."

He boosted her so she could grab a low-hanging branch. She reached up farther and continued to climb. Ryan scrambled up and joined her on a bough that still had a few thick-leaved branches. They watched from their hide as the small squadron of termites swooped over the pigs.

The warthogs were fast runners, some even dodging the aerial assaults. A termite landed on a sow's back and exploded. The animal squealed but didn't go down even though there was an ugly raw wound on its back.

Ryan saw a hog hit a termite head-on that had landed on the ground and then trample over the giant insect, grinding its fragile wings in the dirt.

There was so much squealing, Ryan could only imagine what it might sound like in a slaughterhouse. The melee moved through the damaged jackalberry trees and passed under Ryan and Celeste.

"Now, let's go!" Ryan said.

They jumped down out of the tree and dashed toward the Jeep while the wild pigs bolted in the other direction and the termites returned to their behemoth mound.

Suddenly, Celeste tripped and landed on her face.

Ryan turned and came back. "Are you hurt?"

Her chin was scraped up from the fall. Ryan extended his hand and pulled her to her feet.

That's when they both saw the object that had caused Celeste to trip.

A chunk of igneous rock was embedded in the ground. It was moss green and the size of a medicine ball.

"Holy crap, Ryan. We found one!"

"That's a meteorite?"

"It must have come down through those trees."

"Okay, now can we go look for Ally?"

"Not until we load this in the Jeep. I think I saw a shovel by the rear tire."

"Do you really think that's wise? Bringing this back?"

"Ryan! This is an astronomer's wildest dream!"

44

Vane tugged open the car door. "What are you doing?" he snapped and snatched the tablet out of Ally's hand.

"You murderer!" Ally yelled, glaring up at him.

"It's not what you think."

"You killed all those animals just so you could get your picture with them! What kind of sick person are you?"

"If you'll quit yelling for a second, I'll tell you," Vane said.

"All right, I'm listening."

"Do you know who I am?"

"No, you never told me your name."

"I'm Tyrone Vane."

Ally's eyes widened. "The multi-billionaire?"

"One and the same."

"Just because you're rich doesn't give you the right to go around killing defenseless animals!"

"Well, I wouldn't go so far as calling them defenseless. And what makes you think I killed them?"

"Those pictures on your tablet."

"Here, look again," Vane said and handed the device to Ally.

She swiped her finger across the screen, flipping through the pictures. "They look dead to me."

Vane reached around and grabbed the tranquilizer gun that he'd left leaning up against the front tire. He held the air gun in front of Ally's face. "How do you know they weren't just asleep?"

"You mean..."

"For me, it's just about the thrill of the hunt. Nothing more. And I like to take pictures. Hey, I might be egotistical and love nothing better than to overindulge myself, but I'm really not a bad person."

Ally didn't comment.

Vane glanced up and saw that Sasha had passed out. "If we don't get her out of there, she's going bake to death in that mud."

Ally jumped out of the Land Rover. She ran over to the base of the fallen tree, picked up the makeshift harness hooked to the winch cable, and stepped up onto the trunk. She shuffled along the length of the tree until she was an arm's length away from touching Sasha. She was able to toss the harness and loop it around Sasha's head and under her right front leg on the first try.

"We're ready!" Ally yelled.

Vane was sitting inside the Land Rover. He pressed the button on the handheld winch control and slowly revved the engine. He watched through the windshield as the strung cable became taut and the lioness was pulled out of the mire.

Ally stepped carefully down the trunk, watching to make sure Sasha's head didn't go face down in the muck as she was dragged on top of the boggy surface.

Once Sasha was clear of the pit, Vane continued to tug her slowly across the ground. She was caked with thick mud, and it was drying fast in the insufferable heat.

Vane stopped the winch and backed the Land Rover to the creek. He drove the back tires into the water, turned the vehicle, and towed the lioness into a shallow part of the stream. He edged forward and got back on the shore. He climbed out, went around to the back, and opened the rear cargo door. He grabbed two large towels and walked over to the lioness.

Ally had gotten the cub and brought it over so that it could be with its mother as they waded into the water.

"Here, you can clean her up with these towels," Vane said.

"Aren't you going to help?" Ally asked as she splashed the sleeping lioness with water.

"After I stow the winch," he replied. He removed the harness strap and walked the cable back to the front of the Land Rover, but instead of coiling the line back onto the spool, Vane walked back to the cargo compartment.

He reached in, opened the gun case, and took out the VO Falcon rifle.

45

Ryan stood holding the shovel and looked down at the space rock in the shallow crater. "Is it dangerous?"

"There's minimal radiation, but that's to be expected," Celeste said, studying the meter on the Geiger counter as it made a faint scratchy noise. "It should be okay to handle."

"You're sure?" Ryan said skeptically.

"Yes." Celeste turned off the measuring device.

Ryan stepped down and tapped the smooth rock with the metal blade of the shovel, creating a soft *thunking* sound. "What do you think it's made of?"

"If it was iron, it would have resonated louder. This is organic. Most likely chondrite."

"What's that?"

"Means it's non-metallic. Maybe a piece off an asteroid."

"So those meteor showers we've been seeing, they're all from the same   asteroid."

"Possibly." Celeste looked in the direction of the giant termite mound. "Maybe we should quit talking and get this in the Jeep."

Ryan scooped the dirt out from around the base of the rock to determine its true size. A third of it had impacted into the ground. He kept digging and shoveling out soil until there was enough room to get their hands underneath.

"Watch your back," Ryan said as they both squatted down and grabbed under the rock. "On the count of three—one, two, three!" They straightened their knees and picked up the large rock, which proved to be slightly bigger than a medicine ball.

"If this was made of iron, I doubt we would even be able to lift it," Celeste said as they walked slowly over to the Jeep.

"Let's put it on the rear seat." They sidestepped to the fender and rolled the space rock into the back.

"Whew," Celeste said, brushing off her hands. She climbed into the Jeep.

Ryan got behind the wheel and started the engine. "So, now what?"

"What do you mean?"

"Well, I can see this was all just a ploy to get me to go with you. You have no idea where my sister is."

"I'm sorry, I really didn't mean to deceive you," Celeste said with a guilty look then perked up. "But I wouldn't worry. I'm sure Isoba and your father will find her."

"I hope you're right." Ryan shifted into gear and tromped on the accelerator. The Jeep sped across the rugged terrain. The suspension was so stiff, Ryan kept bouncing out of his seat, and Celeste had to hold on to the dashboard with two hands each time they careened over rough ground.

The grass was a foot high, so it was difficult for Ryan to know if the ground ahead was level, or if he was going to end up putting them into a ditch.

"Ryan, look over there!" Celeste said, pointing to her right.

He turned and saw three pickup trucks parked about half a mile away on a barren ridge that bordered the grassland. There were men carrying burning torches, walking the perimeter, setting fire to the dry grass.

"What are they doing?" Celeste asked.

Ryan spotted a small herd of grazing zebras and realized that the fire was being purposely set to trap the animals.

"They're poachers!" Ryan yelled.

The wildfire spread fast, choking the air with billowing black smoke as the orange flames licked over the combustible vegetation.

The zebras broke into a gallop to escape the approaching inferno.

Ryan turned his attention back to his driving and slammed on the brakes before they went into a gully. He stood up in the Jeep to get a better look. The trench was too steep to cross even for the four-wheeler.

The wall of flames was closing in, leaving behind a scorched and blackened wasteland. He turned and saw a separate fire converging with the other blaze. The flames were so high that he couldn't see the men that had started the fire or their trucks.

Ryan saw a wide swath of grass that hadn't yet been consumed by the flames. It was their only way out. Hopefully they wouldn't be driving into the poachers' trap.

Ryan spun the Jeep around and steered straight for the gap between the raging fires. The zebras, too, were galloping toward the only means of escape.

Ryan raced up between the zebras, trying his best not to run any of them over as they joined the stampede. The six-hundred-pound equines' heavy hooves thundered and kicked up dust as their bodies rammed against both sides of the Jeep.

Fiery embers blew everywhere in the blinding smoke.

A zebra swung its head, bit into Ryan's shirtsleeve, and ripped out a strip with its powerful teeth.

The two fires were about to merge, the flames rising as high as ten feet in the air.

Many of the panic-stricken zebras were running through the flames.

Ryan and Celeste ducked their heads as the Jeep barreled through the wall of fire; their clothes smoldering when they burst out the other side.

Ryan sped away from the inferno to distance themselves from the poachers then stopped the Jeep to pat out still-burning embers on his clothes. Celeste did the same.

Many of the zebras had trills of smoke wafting off their hides as they cantered off in small groups. Gunshots rang out, further scattering the herd.

Celeste consulted the partially melted compass on the dashboard. "If we head that way, it should take us back to the clinic," she said, pointing her finger.

Ryan gunned the Jeep, praying they had enough gas to get back.

46

Ally took a sopping wet towel out of the water and draped it on Sasha. Each time she repeated the process, she was able to dissolve more of the caked-on mud from the lioness's white fur. She placed another towel over the animal and let it soak.

The lion cub contentedly sat on the bank and watched.

Sasha blew out a heavy breath. The sedative was beginning to wear off.

Ally watched the big cat's eyes for the first sign of a fluttering eyelid. It was best to be at a safe distance when the groggy feline came around. Any sign of a threat and the dopey lioness would surely lash out. Ally had no intention of being within reach if that should happen.

She continued to bathe the lioness and was making good progress as most of the mud had washed off.

The right eyelid rose, revealing an amber eye; the diluted pupil just a slit in the middle of the iris.

Ally pulled a saturated towel off of Sasha and wrung it out. She draped the damp fabric over the back of her own neck to cool herself down. She grabbed the other towel, folded it in half, and squeezed the moisture out.

Sasha tossed her head and shook the water out of her ears.

That was Ally's cue to back away. "She's coming to!"

"Excellent," Vane replied from a distance.

Ally turned and saw Vane leaning over the front fender of the Land Rover with his elbows propped on the hood, aiming a hunting rifle at the lioness.

"What are you doing?" Ally yelled, waving her arms in the air and stepping into the line of fire to shield the big cat.

"Move out of the way!"

"No, I won't let you do this." Ally could hear Sasha behind her, splashing in the water as she struggled to get on her feet.

"And how do you plan to stop me?"

"By standing right here. You're not going to shoot me."

"Don't be so sure." Vane stepped back from the vehicle, holding his masterly handcrafted VO Falcon rifle. He took a couple steps so he could get a better angle.

Ally moved and blocked the pathway for the bullet with her body.

"I'm warning you," Vane growled. He edged his way over to the creek and waded into the water up to his knees.

"No! Please don't..." Ally started to plead but stopped when she glanced over her shoulder and saw the menacing five hundred-plus pound lioness stand up and take a step toward her.

Her sense of survival kicked in and she backed toward the shore—in the direction of the lion cub.

Vane grabbed his opportunity and put Sasha in his gun sight. He put his finger inside the trigger guard, took a deep breath, and gently pulled back on the trigger.

A large silver fish with vertical stripes lunged out of the water and sank its one-inch long dagger-like teeth into Vane's right thigh. He screamed and fired into the air as the monstrous fish tore out a meaty chunk from his leg.

Ally saw three more fish attack Vane. They had to be at least 150 pounds each and were lightning fast. They savagely ripped slabs of flesh out of Vane's arms and legs, and dragged him to the bottom. Large gouts of blood floated to the surface.

Then, as fast as they appeared, the powerful fish sped off down the stream, leaving Vane to float up to the surface, facedown in the center of the crimson sheen.

Ally stepped warily out of the creek and turned around.

Sasha and her cub were already leaving, sauntering toward a nearby hill; what remained of her lion pride waiting for them on the crest.

47

Frank was the first to spot Ally. When she saw them coming, she jumped up and down, waving her arms. There was a new model Land Rover parked partially on the bank and in the creek.

"I wonder who that belongs to?" Frank said to Isoba.

"I don't know," Isoba said, "but I've seen it before." He drove past the mud pit and came to a halt next to the other vehicle.

Frank jumped out of the cab and received a big hug from Ally.

"Thank God you're here."

"Sorry we took so long," Frank apologized, putting his arms around his stepdaughter and giving her an assuring squeeze. He looked over and saw a man floating in the creek. "Who's that?"

Ally glanced over her shoulder. "He said his name was Tyrone Vane."

"I've heard of him," Frank said coolly. "What happened, crocodiles?"

"No, they were enormous fish with big teeth."

"What did they look like?"

"They were silver and had stripes."

"Like a tiger," Isoba said.

"Yes, that's correct," Ally said.

"Goliath tiger fish. They are ferocious killers."

"You were lucky they didn't get you," Frank said.

Ally looked over at the Jeep transport and didn't see anyone sitting in the cab. "Are Dr. Tomie and Dayo all right?"

"Yes, we found them last night. They're both recuperating nicely back at the clinic. I feel bad that we had to leave you out here by yourself but Isoba thought it was best we come back in the morning and pick up your trail."

"That's okay, I wasn't alone."

"No?"

"I had the little one to keep me company."

"The little one?" Frank asked.

"Sasha's cub."

"So, you were able to rescue it?"

"That's right."

"Where's it now?"

Ally pointed to a grassy hummock where the entire lion pride was lounging together in the blistering heat.

Frank could see the giant white lioness basking under the sun with her cub. "What exactly happened here?"

Ally explained how Sasha had been trapped in the mud pit and how she and Vane had gotten her free. "He has pictures on his tablet of all these animals he's killed."

"Well, I guess we have one less trophy hunter to worry about, eh, Isoba?"

Isoba was gazing down at the bottom of the creek. "I see his rifle."

"Probably not a good idea to go in the water with those tiger fish around."

"We can always use another rifle," Isboa said.

"You really want that one?" Ally said. "After all the animals it's murdered?"

"No, I suppose not."

"Just leave it. No one's going to want it," Frank said then turned to Ally. "Come on, let's get you back before your mother strings me up by my thumbs."

"Mom wouldn't never do that," Ally said.

"Don't be so sure."

48

Wanda had relieved Adanna from guard duty for a spell so the young woman could get some food, when the Jeep transport pulled into the compound. She stepped away from the crude jailhouse and waved her good arm when she saw Ally step out of the cab.

"Thank God you're okay," she yelled.

Ally ran over. Careful so as not to aggravate her collarbone, Wanda put her arm gingerly around her daughter. With one eye on her prisoner, Wanda listened while Ally told her story about saving the cub and the night in the cave then rescuing Sasha from the mud and the evil game hunter.

"That's incredible. Honey, I'm so glad you're safe," Wanda said, doing her best to hold back the tears.

"Where's Dillon?" Ally asked.

"Dillon and Dayo are feeding Lucy."

Frank had been waiting for the right moment, and when he saw Wanda and Ally both smiling, he ambled over. "I guess Ally told you what happened?"

"She did," Wanda replied. "Thank you for finding her."

"Just part of my job description—first priority: rescue missing daughter."

"You know," Ally said, "there were these *huge* crickets in that cave."

"Sounds like cave crickets; how large were they?" Frank asked.

Ally held the palms of her hands twelve inches apart.

"Are you serious?" Wanda said.

"That can't be right."

"I swear they were that big."

Wanda noticed the perplexed look on Frank's face.

"That's not all," Ally continued. "When I found Sasha trapped in the mud, there were these giant wasps."

"Were they black with yellows legs?" Frank asked.

"Yes, how did you know?"

"They were most likely mud daubers. How big were *they*?"

"Bigger than me."

"Jesus, Frank," Wanda said. "What's going on around here?"

"I don't know, but I'd sure like to find out."

Isoba came over and was drinking water from a metal cup that he had fetched from the kitchen. "I will watch the prisoner now," he said to Wanda. "You should be with your daughter."

"Thank you, Isoba," Wanda said and smiled as the man went and sat in the chair a few feet from Duna, who was slumped behind the bars of his converted cell.

"What's Ryan up to?" Frank asked.

"I don't know. The Willys is gone, so I'm assuming he and Celeste went off somewhere."

"When did they leave?"

"I have no idea," Wanda said. "I hope he hasn't gone and got himself lost. I don't know if I can take much more of this; first Ally, now him. What if they don't come back by nightfall?"

"Well, you did say that Ryan and Celeste went together. I doubt if they would get lost. Celeste can navigate her way back using the stars."

Wanda let out a forced laugh. "Yeah, I forgot. Silly me."

"If it will make you feel any better, I'll go look for him. Let me go grab a quick bite and a cool drink."

"I'm sorry, I don't mean to sound like..." but then Wanda paused when she heard the approaching engine as the Willys Jeep raced into the compound.

Ryan slammed on the brakes, kicking up a cloud of dust.

"Hey, slow down," Frank said, waving his hand in front of his face.

"We found one!" Celeste shouted excitedly.

"Found what? Wanda asked.

"A meteorite!"

"Great! Let's get it inside," Frank said.

49

Dr. Tomie suggested that it was important they take certain precautions while examining the meteorite. The first was limiting access. It was decided that only the veterinarian, Frank, and Celeste would be allowed in the room. The three wore surgical masks and gloves, along with plastic protective clothing that Dr. Tomie kept on hand whenever it was necessary to form a team to evaluate contagious outbreaks in the savanna.

"How do you think we should proceed?" Dr. Tomie said, gazing down at the meteorite lying on the table. Her right foot was slightly raised off the floor as she shifted some of her weight on the single crutch tucked under her armpit.

"Why don't we give Celeste the lead on this," Frank said.

"Very well. Celeste?"

The young woman was studying the solid piece of space debris with a magnifying glass. "Well, when we first found it, I thought it was just ordinary chondrite, which is the composite of eighty percent of all meteorites found, " she said and looked up. "But now that I'm able to get a closer look at this one, I'm not so sure."

"What do you think it is?" Frank asked. He put his hand out and Celeste passed him the magnifying glass so he could take a look.

"Well, there are several types of meteorites. Achondrites have stony crusts. This one is porous, almost like hardened magma. I don't see any gem-like crystals, so we can rule out it being a pallasite. It's too bad we don't have a mass spectrometer. I'd love to know how old it is."

"What if you were to guess?" Dr. Tomie said.

"It could be a million years old, maybe a billion, who knows."

"A lot could happen in that amount of time. Hell, this thing could have traveled the entire galaxy," Frank said. "And back."

"Possibly. I believe it originated from the asteroid belt that Earth has been passing through for the past three years," Celeste said. "I'd like to get a sample and examine it under a microscope."

"You mean break off a piece?" Frank said.

"Do we really want to do that?" Dr. Tomie said, voicing her concern along with Frank's.

"The spot where Ryan and I found this meteorite, there were also gigantic termites."

"Isoba and I encountered an emperor scorpion the size of an SUV at the village," Frank said. "Abnormally large insects are popping up everywhere."

"Yeah, well, those stupid termites were actually blowing themselves up."

"You two were lucky you didn't get sprayed by the toxin. It's known as *autothysis* or suicidal altruism. They're able to rupture an organ and explode at will. Pretty amazing stuff."

"I believe these meteorites are the direct cause of the mutations."

Frank looked at Dr. Tomie. "What do you say?"

"If Celeste is right, then we have no choice but to see what's inside this thing."

Using her crutch, Dr. Tomie hobbled across the room. She stopped, reached in a drawer, and took out a small surgical chisel and a light ball-peen hammer. "Anywhere in particular?" she asked Celeste.

"Yes, try here." Celeste pointed to a small bump on the rock and stepped back to make room for the veterinarian.

"Would you like me to do that?" Frank asked.

"Frank, if I can remove a lion's canines, I think I can chip off a little piece of rock."

"Be my guest."

Dr. Tomie leaned on her crutch. She put the tip of the chisel at the base of the protrusion, tapped the end with the head of the hammer, and chipped off a tiny sliver, which fell on the tabletop.

"Very nice," Frank replied. "May I?"

Dr. Tomie nodded. She pointed to the microscope on the counter next to the sink.

Frank picked up the rock chip, walked over, and placed the sample on a glass slide under the revolving three-lens nosepiece. After turning on the illuminator, he bent over and stared into the eyepiece.

A few seconds later, he reached down, repositioned the fragment and twisted the lens to the next magnification. "This is incredible."

"What do you see?" Celeste asked, stepping over as Dr. Tomie limped to stand behind Frank.

"One sec," Frank said. He flipped to the 200x magnification setting and adjusted the focus knob.

The porous rock looked like giant craters on the moon. Bizarre-looking, microscopic creatures resided in the deep depressions.

They must have ducked out of sight when he had made his sweep with the magnifying glass. The microorganisms were so small they blended with the rock and were practically undetectable by the naked eye unless someone knew what to look for.

Their gray translucent bodies were thin and elliptic. Each one had a single pulsing orifice in the center of its domed head. Frank couldn't tell if they were mouths or sex organs.

The oviform organisms had weird squid-like tentacles that looked like short Chinese glass noodles with tiny barbs on the ends for clutching the rock.

They didn't appear at all threatening; on the contrary, they looked more like something a fisherman might bait on a hook.

Frank stood up straight and took a step back. "You're not going to believe this."

Celeste peered through the eyepiece. "Oh my God! They're alive!"

"Let me see," Dr. Tomie said and took her turn. She studied the slide for almost a minute before raising her head. She turned around and leaned up against the counter.

"Well, what do you think?" Frank asked.

"Definitely a microorganism," Dr. Tomie said.

"True, but nothing I've ever seen before."

"Me neither."

"So we're definitely looking at an alien life form," Celeste said.

"That would be my guess," Frank said. "You may be right, Celeste. They might be what's been triggering these strange insect anomalies."

"But why does it only affect some and not the others?" Dr. Tomie said.

"I think there's only one way to find out," Frank said.

"And how's that?"

"We'll need to run an experiment."

50

Frank returned to the examining room, carrying a small, clear plastic Petri dish with a perforated lid.

"What did you find?" Dr. Tomie asked. She had grown tired trying to stand on one foot and was sitting on a stool with casters.

"Well, I walked the compound and came across a few straggler safari ants and a couple scorpions," Frank said, "but after our past run-ins decided they weren't our ideal test subjects. I did come across a *Scytodes thoracica* hiding under one of the railings."

"A what?" Celeste asked.

"A spitting spider. They don't bite so they're relatively harmless."

"You said *relatively* harmless," Dr. Tomie said.

"Well, they do have the ability to spit out a sticky venomous web and actually lasso their prey."

"You couldn't find anything else?" Dr. Tomie asked.

"I could go back out and look."

Celeste stared at the diminutive spider trapped inside the Petri dish. The round head and the orb body were brown with tiny black markings. Its legs had the same coloring and were long and extremely thin. "I think it should be all right. It doesn't look that tough."

"Okay, let's see what happens," Frank said. He walked over to the microscope and removed the sample of the meteorite from the slide. He twisted off the cap on the Petri dish and carefully slipped the sliver of rock inside. He quickly replaced the lid before the spider could escape.

Frank placed the shallow, cylindrical dish on top of the slide. He leaned down and peered through the eyepiece.

Dr. Tomie and Celeste gathered round anxiously, waiting their turn.

A minute had passed, then two before Frank announced, "The spider is about to...whoa!"

"What happened?" Celeste said.

"One of those organisms was squeezing out of the rock and the spitting spider immobilized it with its web."

"Let me take a look." Celeste waited for Frank to move aside then gazed into the eyepiece.

Dr. Tomie hopped over and braced against the counter as she took her turn at the microscope. "The other organisms seem to be retreating."

"May I?" Frank asked. He held onto Dr. Tomie's elbow and helped her back to the stool. He turned and peered into the eyepiece. "You're right, they're scurrying back into their holes."

"Seems they'd rather stay put in their natural habitat than venture into our world," Dr. Tomie said.

"Maybe they're just shy," Celeste said and smiled.

"More like part of their defense mechanism," Frank said, still looking through the eyepiece. "Wait a minute... oh my gosh, the spider is eating the one it caught in its web."

"Frank, could it be that those insects that mutated, ate one of these organisms?"

"Might explain why only a few have been affected. Let's pray these little space pests stay homebound."

"Wait a minute, you two," Celeste interjected. "What about the spider? Isn't it going to turn into one of those giant bugs?"

"Damn!" Frank said as he took another look through the lens piece.

"What's wrong?" Dr. Tomie asked.

"The spider isn't moving. I think it's dead." Frank lifted the Petri dish off of the stage and placed it on the counter. He removed the lid slowly and everyone gazed at the motionless spider. "I don't get it."

"How strange," Celeste said.

Frank took a pen out of his shirt pocket and prodded the limp spider with the ballpoint tip, but the arachnid remained wilted and didn't move.

"Looks like our little experiment just went kaput," Dr. Tomie said.

Frank replaced the lid. "Is it all right if I put our recently deceased little friend in your supply frig? I'd like to take another look at it a little later."

"Sure, it's over there," Dr. Tomie said and pointed to a small, single-door commercial refrigerator in the corner of the room. She waited until Frank had put the Petri dish on a metal rack and closed the door before saying, "You know, I'd feel better if we got this outside," gesturing to the meteorite. "Especially now that we know what's crawling around inside."

"You're right."

"Wait a minute," Celeste protested. "I was hoping to study it a bit more."

"I'm sorry, but it's too dangerous to keep in here," Dr. Tomie said. "How do we know these things aren't a threat to us? I mean, if our theory is right, and these things can drastically alter a creature's metabolism..."

"I agree," Frank said. "We'll take it somewhere not too far away. You can conduct your study there."

"Sounds fair enough. As Ryan and I brought it here, I'd like him to drive me."

"I don't know," Frank replied, concerned for their safety.

"Nothing happened before. I'm sure we'll be okay. As soon as we drop it off, we'll come right back. I promise."

"Okay, then."

"Great! I'll go get Ryan," Celeste said and rushed off.

"You know, Frank," Dr. Tomie said. "Something's been bothering me."

"What's that, Gayle?"

"All these meteor showers we've been having. Are these things in all of them?"

"What are you suggesting?" Frank said.

"Could this be an invasion?"

51

Frank helped Ryan carry the meteorite out to the Willys Jeep. As an added precaution, Frank had bundled the space rock up in a canvas tarp and sealed the edges with a heavy-duty stapler Dr. Tomie kept in her office. Celeste had gone inside the clinic to use the restroom.

"You know, I shouldn't let you do this," Frank said. "Your mother was worried sick the last time you took off."

"I know, I'm sorry. Trust me, we won't go far." Ryan had a worried look on his face.

"What's wrong?" Frank asked. "Oh, I guess Celeste told you about what's in that rock."

"About those things? Yeah, but that's not it."

"What then?"

"When we were coming back we crossed paths with some poachers. They were trying to burn out the animals."

"Why didn't you mention this before?"

"Like you said, I didn't want to worry Mom."

"Then it's settled," Frank said. "I'm going with you."

"Good. They were pretty scary."

"You can fill me in on the details while we drive. Hang tight while I go grab a gun." Frank dashed inside the building and saw Wanda and Isoba walking down the corridor. "Isoba!"

Isoba turned and faced Frank. "Yes, Mr. Travis."

"I need one of your rifles."

"What for?' Wanda asked.

"I'm accompanying Ryan and Celeste while we dispose of that meteorite."

"What, you suspect trouble?"

"Ryan said the last time they were out, they saw poachers."

"Did he say how many?" Isoba asked.

"No."

"It has to be Abrafo. He is coming for his brother."

"Then I suggest you guys get everyone armed and ready," Frank said.

Wanda grabbed Frank's arm. "You *really* have to go out there?"

"We won't be long."

"Be careful."

"We will." Frank kissed Wanda and looked at Isoba. "I'll need that weapon."

They rushed down the hall to the gunroom. Isoba unlocked the door and the cage, and handed Frank a 30-06 Weatherby Mark V bolt-action rifle—a firearm that Frank was familiar with—and a box of shells.

Wanda and Isoba were already discussing how they were going to fortify the clinic when Frank dashed down the passageway and out the door. Ryan and Celeste were already in the Willys Jeep, waiting with the engine running. Celeste was squished behind the passenger seat and the covered meteorite.

Frank jumped into the Jeep. He stood the rifle between his legs and held the ammo box on his lap. "We better make this fast. Isoba thinks those poachers you guys saw are coming for Duna."

Ryan stepped on the gas and they raced out of the compound.

52

Wanda and Isoba stood on the observation deck overlooking the savanna and could see two trucks parked on the opposite shore of the small lake.

"I count seven, but there could be more," Wanda said and passed the binoculars over to Isoba. He took a quick look and lowered the binoculars. "The tall one in the yellow shirt..."

"Yes, standing by the driver's door of the blue truck."

"That is Abrafo."

"So he's their leader," Wanda said. "Chances are, we take him out first, the others won't bother to attack."

"Some of them are Duna's men. They won't stop until they have freed their boss."

"So what can we expect?" Wanda asked.

"They will have automatic rifles and maybe pistols. Some will carry hatchets and machetes. They will kill everyone here."

"This goes against my credo, but maybe we should just hand over Duna. I don't like putting my family in danger."

Isoba shook his head. "It would do no good. They would just come back later and finish the job."

"Well, looks like they're not giving us much of a choice," Wanda said. "Let's go inside and round everyone up. We better be ready when they come."

53

"There's a good spot," Celeste said, directing Ryan's attention to a small stand of trees. Ryan cut the wheel sharply, causing Frank to spill the entire box of shells onto the floor mat. Frank cursed, reaching down to grab a few bullets just as Ryan straightened the wheel, sending the cartridges rolling under his seat. He'd only managed to load a couple bullets into the hunting rifle's magazine before popping in the clip.

Ryan slammed on the brakes. Frank saw a few cartridges roll out from under the seat just as he grabbed the dashboard so he wouldn't catapult over the folded down windshield and land face first on the hood. Celeste didn't fare any better as the meteorite shifted due to the abrupt stop, pressing her against the side of the Jeep.

"Could you guys please get this off of me," she pleaded.

Ryan jumped out first and came around to the rear of the Jeep. Frank got out and leaned the rifle against the back fender. They lifted the rock off the rear seat and shuffled under the shade of the nearest tree.

As they were stooping to put the rock down, Frank caught a glimpse of a truck parked behind the trees. A man came out of nowhere and smashed Frank on the side of the head with the butt stock of his AK-47.

Frank immediately dropped to his knees.

"Hey, what the—" Ryan never got to finish his sentence as another man appeared and punched him in the face. He fell on the ground next to his stepfather.

Celeste screamed from the Jeep.

Frank winced when his assailant kicked him in the ribs. He looked up. A third man was molesting Celeste, forcing her down on the back seat.

Their barbaric attackers were shirtless and sweaty, wearing filthy baggy pants and sandals. They look crazed and violent. The two poachers who had assaulted Frank and Ryan were wearing sheathed machetes.

The one with the assault rifle struck Ryan between the shoulder blades with the butt stock, knocking the wind out of the young man and forcing him to gasp for air.

Each man grabbed one of Ryan's hands by the wrists and they hauled him over to a tree stump.

Celeste continued to scream as the man ripped her clothes.

One man pinned Ryan down and draped his right arm over the flat stump. The other man put his assault rifle down, pulled out his machete, and raised the rusty blade over his head.

Eyes on the Jeep, Frank crawled for his rifle.

That's when he heard Ryan scream, "No, God, please don't…"

54

Wanda glanced out the back door of the clinic. It was nearly nightfall. She heard an engine and ducked back just as the first truck pulled up in the compound. Three men climbed out of the cab. The two that were carrying machetes were average height and weight, but the third man was short and tubby, well over two hundred pounds. He was armed with a handgun.

They headed toward the open doorway.

Stepping backward down the gloomy hallway—a defense tactic had been to unscrew all of the overhead light bulbs—Wanda went around a corner and got into position.

She could hear the men entering the building, talking in low whispers. She hunkered down in the shadows. Everything seemed eerily quiet. She figured the three who came into the clinic were instructed to massacre everyone inside.

Abrafo and the other three poachers were most likely combing the perimeter outside and searching the cottages for Duna. Wanda knew eventually they would get to the animal enclosures. Even though Duna was bound and gagged, it was doubtful if Isoba could keep him quiet and hidden for long.

Sooner or later they would find Duna.

Wanda could tell by their footsteps that they were splitting up to widen their search of the building, which she had counted on them doing. She could hear one coming her way.

She waited until the man was only ten feet away before stepping out from her hiding place. "That's far enough!"

The man stopped, surprised by her bold move. Here was an injured woman with her arm in a sling, ready to oppose him. How stupid could she be? He looked her up and down then sneered and raised his machete, ready to rush her.

"Don't say I didn't warn you," Wanda said. She turned sideways with her arm in the sling facing the intruder.

The poacher yelled something in his language and charged.

Three bright muzzle flashes lit up the hallway as Wanda pulled the trigger on the Beretta concealed in her sling. The rapid fire pelted the man in the chest and sent him flying onto the floor.

***

Adanna could hear heavy breathing like a water buffalo laboring up a hill. Armed with a sawed-off shotgun, she hid behind a door that was slightly ajar so she could see anyone coming down the dark corridor. Judging by the approaching man's silhouette, he was rotund and twice her weight. But that didn't alarm her. Once he was close enough, she would step out from behind the door and cut him down to size with the scattergun.

Two shots fired in the gloom.

Adanna ducked.

The bullets ripped holes in the door, missing her head by mere inches.

Adanna kicked the door back and fired off a blast of buckshot. The pellets sprayed the wall. But the man wasn't there. He had stepped back out of the line of fire.

A beefy hand reached out and grabbed the barrel of Adanna's shotgun and ripped the weapon right out of her hands. Then a fist came out of nowhere and clipped her across the jawbone. She went staggering back and landed flat on her butt.

The portly man lumbered over and kicked her in the chest with his broad foot.

Adanna fell back, and before she knew what was happening, the heavy man was sitting on her chest with his thick, sausage fingers around her throat.

Adanna couldn't reach up to pry his fingers away because the man had her arms pinned under his knees. She could feel her airway closing, kinking like a twisted tube, and her head went woozy...

"Get off my sister!"

The man turned and looked up.

A white blur pummeled his face, smashing his nose into mush. He threw back his head and roared with rage. He released his grip so that he could push himself up from the floor.

Adanna took in a deep gasping breath. As the man struggled to get to his feet, she reached over and snatched the shotgun off the floor. Raising the barrel, she aimed for the man's back and pulled the trigger. At such close range, the cluster of lead riddled his spine. His legs turned to jelly and he belly-flopped on the floor.

Wasting no time, Adanna got back on her feet. She gazed at the person standing in front of her. "That was some hit."

"Yes it was," Dayo said. "Broke my cast."

***

"Someone's shooting," Dillon said.

"Quiet, they'll hear you," Ally snapped at her little brother and put her hand over his mouth. They were hiding under the table in the examination room. A large sheet was draped over the front so they couldn't be seen by anyone entering the room.

"Ummph," Dillon mumbled, pulling Ally hand away. "Hey..."

"Shh, I hear something."

There was a creak as the door opened, followed by footfalls entering the room.

Ally and Dillon looked at each other, afraid to breathe.

Dillon closed his eyes.

Ally's head cocked as she tried to figure out where the interloper was based on his sounds as he crept about the room.

After enduring agonizing seconds thinking they were going to be discovered, the door creaked, signally that the prowler was leaving.

Ally and Dillon were too scared to move. Finally, Dillon said, "See, I told you they wouldn't..."

The sheet flew up and an ugly man with a scar across his cheek and rotted teeth grinned when he made Ally and Dillon scream.

55

The poacher standing over Ryan was about to come down with his machete when a loud buzzing emanated from the trees. He and the man holding Ryan by the wrist turned to see what was causing the strange sound. The man straddling Celeste was also drawn by the strange reverberation and sat back on his haunches to take a look.

Lying on the ground and not far from the Jeep—and his rifle—Frank was quite familiar with the sound, having listened to countless tape recordings and conducting lengthy research on the highly aggressive species. He had even developed a three-hour lesson plan for his students on this specific animal.

This particular order of insect was so deadly in large numbers, they could easily kill a horse. Judging by the stentorian hum, the swarm had to be enormous.

Imagine his surprise when three Africanized killer bees flew out of the trees.

The bees were as big as the Willys Jeep—only with two sets of wings.

The man about to chop off Ryan's arm dropped his machete and scooped up his AK-47. He pulled back the operating rod, released the handle, and the bolt slammed forward, feeding a round into the chamber—all of which took two precious seconds, enough time for one of the bees to buzz down and snatch him off the ground.

Frank looked up as the man was hauled into the air. The man jammed the muzzle of his assault rife into the bee's underbelly and fired off a quick succession of bullets that ripped the bee's abdomen apart in an eruption of silver tracheal gore. The act gave the man the opportunity to escape the clutches of his captor. If only he hadn't been fifty feet in the air.

The man screamed all the way down, plummeting to the ground. He hit just as the enormous bee splattered on top of his dead body.

A giant bee swooped over the Jeep and latched onto Celeste's attacker. The man yelled, flailing his arms to break free as the mid-tibia spurs on the bee's six legs used for collecting pollen, pierced his flesh. The bee tucked the end of its abdomen and drove its curved stinger into the man's back, the tip sticking clear out of his chest and still shooting out venom.

But when the bee attempted to take flight, the man slipped from its clutches. As he fell away, the connected stinger ripped out from the end of the bee's abdomen, followed by a long, gooey gut-strand. The two crashed to the ground.

The last bee was hovering over Ryan and the poacher by the stump.

Frank crawled over to the Jeep. He grabbed his rifle, aimed the gun, and pulled the trigger.

The high-caliber bullet punched a hole in the poacher's chest and exited out his back in a red spurt.

"Ryan! Get over here!" Frank yelled. He drew back the bolt to insert the next shell into the chamber and closed the breech. He put the giant bee in his sights and pulled the trigger.

Nothing happened.

There should have been another round in the clip. He looked down at the ground and saw that the magazine had fallen out.

Ryan rushed past him and jumped behind the wheel. Celeste had crawled into the front passenger seat, so Frank vaulted in the back.

Firing up the engine, Ryan drove off while Frank frantically felt around the floor for a loose cartridge that he could load into the gun.

The Jeep raced across the uneven terrain, bouncing like a racecar slamming over a series of jarring speed bumps.

Celeste screamed and Frank looked up at the enormous striped underbelly over his head.

The giant bee seized Celeste by the shoulders.

Frank grabbed her by the waist to anchor her down. He could feel the forceful downdraft of the bee's mighty wings beating on his face.

Ryan kept one hand on the wheel and grasped Celeste by her ripped shirt.

"Don't let me go!" Celeste screamed.

Frank could feel his grip slipping.

The bee was incredibly strong and lifted Celeste off the seat.

"I can't hold on!" Ryan yelled as a piece of Celeste's shirt tore off in his hand.

A dark shadow swooped over the Jeep and the bee suddenly released Celeste, who fell back in her seat.

"What the hell is that?" Ryan gasped as he slowed down the Jeep.

Frank gazed in amazement as the heinous creature darted with its prey for the closest tree. The bee's abductor was slightly larger with primarily blue coloring on its head, legs, and wings. It hooked a leg on a thick bough and dangled holding its catch, driving its spear-like proboscis deep into the bee's thorax. "You're looking at a species from the *Asilidae* family or what's commonly called a robber fly, which is known to hunt prey equal to its own size."

"Thank God for that," Celeste said, quite shaken up.

"That's sick," Ryan said, watching the bee shrivel up as the grotesque robber fly sucked the body fluids out with its long proboscis.

Frank was about to agree when he heard distant gunfire. "The clinic's under attack!" He reached down for the box of bullets but was thrown back against the seat when Ryan tromped on the accelerator.

.

56

The poacher tried to drag Dillon out from under the examining table but Ally held on fast to her brother's other arm. "Let him go!" she hollered.

The man was relentless and kept yanking. Ally thought for sure he was going to rip Dillon's arm out of the socket, especially the way Dillon was yelling.

Rather than have her brother injured, Ally let go and the poacher fell back on the floor.

Ally scurried out the other side, grabbed the edge of the gurney, and ran it across the room. The underside cleared Dillon's head as he was on his knees but the edge of the rolling table rammed into the man's head as he was getting up and knocked him back down.

"Dillon, grab my hand!" Ally reached for her brother.

The scowling poacher got up, snatched Dillon by the back of his shirt, and stood blocking the doorway.

"Leave my brother—" Ally turned when she heard a loud thud in the corner of the room. It was coming from the refrigerator.

Again, something pounded on the inside of the door like it was trying to get out.

Curiosity got the better of the man. He dragged Dillon along and crossed the room to see what was inside. Before he could reach for the handle, the fridge door burst open.

Ally couldn't believe her eyes. It was a giant brown spider. It was hard to imagine it could even fit in such close quarters when it stretched out and stood on its spindly legs.

The arachnid's head and body were as big as jumbo-size beach balls, and it was six feet tall standing on its stilt-like appendages.

The poacher was too scared to move, giving Dillon the chance he needed to run over and hide behind his sister.

Ally couldn't tell if the six black eyes on the spider's head were looking at her or the frightened man. The creature swayed side to the side, not so much to keep its balance as preparing to lunge. She stepped back, bumping Dillon against the wall just as the spider spit out long, continuous strings of white silk from its mouth.

The poacher screamed as the crisscrossing patterns of silk singed his flesh and enveloped his head and torso like a cocoon.

***

Ryan pulled into the compound next to the poachers' truck and they all jumped out. Frank, the only one with a gun, led the way inside the dark clinic.

This time there was a bullet in the chamber and three in the magazine.

They went down a back hall and found a dead man lying on the floor. Someone was standing at the junction, which led down the unlit corridor to the examination room.

Frank raised his rifle. "Who's there?"

"It's me," Wanda replied.

"Are you guys okay?"

Two other figures stepped out of the gloom.

Frank trained his gun in their direction.

"It's us, Dayo and Adanna," Adanna said.

"Where're Ally and Dillon?" Frank asked.

"Hiding in the examination room," Wanda replied.

"And Dr. Tomie?"

"I'm not sure."

"We'll go look for her," Ryan said. He and Celeste went down the hall toward the veterinarian's office.

"Come on," Frank said to Wanda. "Let's go get Ally and Dillon."

Frank groped in the dark until they reached the end of the hall. "Where are the lights?"

"Reach up, screw in the bulb," Wanda replied.

Frank felt around until he felt the glass globe and twisted it all the way into the socket until bright light illuminated the passageway. He glanced over at the observation window that faced into the examination room. He could see Ally and Dillon huddled a few feet from the door.

"Oh, my God, Frank," Wanda yelled out when she saw the giant spider cornering her children.

Frank yanked open the door and stepped into the room.

The spider sensed a new prey and sidestepped around to shoot its incapacitating propellant.

Wanda didn't give it a chance and opened fire with her Beretta, each shot punching a hole in the sphere-shaped carapace.

Frank leveled his rifle and blasted the thing in the head until it fell on the floor.

The unrecognizable mass looked like bug splatter on a windshield.

Ally and Dillon ran up to their mom and they all hugged while Frank stared down at the slimy mess on the floor.

Frank turned when Celeste came into the room.

"Oh my," she said, once she saw the gore splattered everywhere.

"Where's Ryan?" Wanda asked as Ally and Dillon stepped back from their mother.

"He's with Dr. Tomie in the gunroom." Celeste looked at Frank. "Is this the same spider?"

"I believe so. Seems it didn't die after all," Frank said. "After it ate the alien life form it must have gone into a dormant stage and metabolized later while it was in the fridge."

"Did you say alien life form?" Wanda asked, bewildered.

"Yeah, they're in the meteorites," Celeste said.

Wanda gave Frank an incredulous look and laughed. "And this is the first I'm hearing of this?"

"Sorry, dear, but it been a little hectic."

"You're telling me."

"So what, is this some type of invasion?"

"Gayle seems to think so," Frank said.

Wanda glanced around the room. "Where're Ally and Dillon?"

57

"Will you wait up?" Ally called out as she chased after her little brother, keeping her voice down just in case there were more of the poachers skulking around. Dillon ran down the tenebrous hall and out the back door.

Ally rushed after him into the dark. There was a sliver of moon etched in the night sky so she could make out shapes. She heard small footfalls near the pens and knew instantly why Dillon had run off. He was worried about Lucy.

She crept along the outer railing of the corrals and edged toward Lucy's stall.

"Dillon!" she whispered sharply.

"We're in here," he answered.

Ally pushed the gate open and snuck in the enclosure. Dillon was standing beside Lucy at the end of the stall. She seemed restless so he was rubbing her side to calm her down. The baby rhino nestled her head against Dillon, content to have the boy's company.

"She was scared," Dillon said, justifying why he had run off.

"Dillon, it's dangerous out here. There are..." but then she clammed up when she heard movement out in the compound.

Shuffling footsteps.

Coming their way.

"Shhh," Ally whispered. She hunkered down with Lucy and Dillon. That's when she realized she had left the gate open—an open invitation for whoever was out there.

A bright light shone in their faces.

Instantly alarmed, Lucy let out a high-pitched, dolphin-like cry.

Ally shielded her eyes and could see the silhouette of the man holding the flashlight. She crouched in front of Dillon to protect her brother.

The man lowered the flashlight slightly so that the beam was shining on the ground as he slipped into the stall.

Ally could see something in his right hand. A hatchet.

"Get away!" Ally shouted.

"Yeah, leave us alone!" Dillon yelled at the man.

Lucy snorted and her right hoof stomped the ground.

Ally watched in horror as the man raised his hatchet and was about to take another step when suddenly there was raucous laughter. At first, she thought the demented chuckling was coming from the man, but then she saw him looking around, equally baffled by the boisterous cackling.

Then she spotted something stumble through the gate and come up behind the poacher.

Ally heard a bone-pulverizing crunch.

The man screamed and dropped both the flashlight and the hatchet. He fell forward on the ground, digging his fingers into the dirt, obviously in a great amount of pain.

Hobbie's head was bent over the man's right leg. The carnivore's jaws were closing like a vise around the back of the kneecap, making a sound like concrete breaking up in a grinder.

The three-legged hyena was remorseless and chomped off the leg.

Blood gushed out of the stump onto the lower portion of the severed limb lying in the ichor-drenched dirt.

The man passed out from the shock, soon to be dead.

Ally grabbed the flashlight and switched it off.

There was no telling how many more were out there.

58

Isoba heard a man scream from somewhere out in the compound. He stayed back in the shadows with his rifle ready, inside the stucco animal enclosure. Duna was bound and gagged next to him. The boss man was determined to free himself and struggled to undo his tied hands.

"Be still," Isoba said and jabbed the rifle muzzle into Duna's ribs.

Duna glared at his captor, his grumbling muffled as he protested with the bandana covering his mouth.

"Quiet," Isoba warned and jabbed his prisoner a second time.

This time Duna became quiet but kept staring malevolently at Isoba.

"Duna!" a voice called out in the dark.

Isoba glanced through the steel bars of the locked door and saw a figure standing twenty feet away. Even though it was dark, he could tell the man was carrying a rifle. The man began walking toward Isoba's hiding place.

Each step the man took, Isoba inched the barrel of his rifle farther out between the bars getting ready to fire. He put his cheek on the stock and looked over the sights to line up the shot, aiming for the man's chest.

Then he was kicked in the back from behind and thrust against the door.

A hand from outside ripped the rifle out of Isoba's hands, pulling the weapon out through the bars.

Isoba rolled on his side and looked up just as Duna kicked him in the face with both bound feet. Before Isoba could react, Duna had already snatched the cell key and was tossing it to the man outside so he could unlock the door.

The key jangled in the lock and the heavy door swung open, banging against the clay wall.

A man entered the tight quarters and quickly cut Duna loose. They grabbed Isoba and dragged him outside and threw him down on the dirt.

Isoba looked up at the three men standing over him. He could see their faces in the weak moonlight and recognized Abrafo.

"I want to kill him," Duna said to his brother.

"Then do it," Abrafo said.

Duna looked at the other man who had only been armed with a machete before snatching away Isoba's gun and helping Duna escape. Duna put out his hand for Isoba's weapon. The man didn't object and handed over the rifle.

"Sooner or later, you will be stopped," Isoba said.

"Not by you," Duna replied and aimed the gun at Isoba's head.

But before the evil poacher could pull the trigger, a woman's voice called out Abrafo's name.

Isoba looked across the yard and saw Dr. Tomie standing just outside the rear door of the clinic. She was leaning on a pair of crutches, though the left one she was using to support herself looked a little irregular.

"You are as foolish as was your husband," Abrafo said.

Isoba was surprised to see Wanda step outside and stand beside the doctor.

Abrafo and Duna both laughed when they saw that the other woman had her arm in a sling.

"You think we are afraid of two crippled women?" Abrafo said.

"As soon as he is dead," Duna said, looking down at Isoba, "I will enjoy killing you next."

"I don't think so," Dr. Tomie said. She swung up her left crutch, pointed the end at Abrafo, and a fiery flash came out the end.

It was then Isoba realized that the crutch was really a rifle.

The bullet smacked Abrafo in the forehead and carried his brains out the hole in the back of his skull.

The poacher with the machete dove and grabbed Abrafo's rifle off the ground. Wanda pulled her Beretta out of the sling and center shot the man in the chest.

Duna turned the barrel of his gun on Isoba, but Isoba was ready and grabbed the muzzle. He pushed the gun barrel away so that the end was pointing at Duna's right foot, and then yanked down so that it was Duna pulling the trigger and the one blowing off his own toes.

Duna yowled and scampered off toward the open gate. A huge shape charged out of the shadows and tackled him to the ground. Duna thrashed about, kicking his feet, his screams muffled by savage growls.

It wasn't long before Duna stopped screaming.

Isoba watched as the Anatolian shepherd came out of the gloom, pranced over to Dr. Tomie, and sat obediently at her side. She reached down and patted the dog on the head.

"Good boy, Samson."

59

Instead of waiting until daybreak, Frank and Isoba decided to dispose of the bodies during the much-cooler night. Frank's first thought was that they should bury the men, but Isoba quickly rebutted, saying they were not deserving of a proper burial. Isoba thought it would be more fitting if the animals were given their justice.

So instead of digging a mass grave, Frank and Isoba hauled the bodies in the transport Jeep a fair distance from the clinic and dumped the corpses in a ravine.

The gruesome ordeal had taken them three hours.

After some sleep, Frank went to Dr. Tomie's office later the next morning. He leaned against the doorjamb and gazed in at Isoba and Celeste, who were sitting at a small table behind the doctor's desk. Celeste had a microphone up to her mouth and was clicking the button while Isoba fiddled with the knobs on the ham radio.

"Any luck?" Frank asked. For some reason their cell phones and Internet devices were not working, and they were unable to get service.

"The signal isn't strong," Celeste said. "But we did hear someone cutting in and out."

"Maybe the park rangers," Isoba said.

"I told them it was imperative that I be airlifted out," Celeste said.

Frank turned as Wanda joined him in the doorway.

"What about the rest of us?" Wanda said indignantly.

"I'm sorry if that sounded a little harsh, but it's important that I get back to my observatory."

"And why's that?" Wanda asked, still a little miffed.

"Remember I told you I've been recording these meteor showers for the past three years?"

"Yes."

"Well, some other astronomers and I have established a network tracking system linked with every observatory around the world. Which means that we have currently pinpointed the locations of every meteorite that has struck our planet so far."

"That would be invaluable information," Frank agreed. "If we destroy the meteorites, we eliminate the alien threat."

"Exactly. Now you see why I have to get out of here."

Wanda nodded. "I understand."

"I'm sure when they come for me there'll be room for all of you."

"Let's hope so," Frank said.

"So this is great news, right?" Wanda said. "Once Celeste and the others relay the locations to the military, the meteorites can all be destroyed."

"Well, don't forget the insects that have already been affected," Frank said.

"Why, they'll all be dead soon. Bugs don't live long."

"Some do, some don't. Sure, flies and wasps live only about thirty days. Crickets maybe three months. But it's the other species that we really need to worry about. Scorpions can live up to fifteen years, some spiders twenty-five years. And if we're talking about a queen, like a termite, you're looking at a lifespan of fifty years."

"Are you serious? Fifty years?" Wanda said, flabbergasted. "But what if—"

"If one of those mutations laid eggs, it would be catastrophic."

60

After the family ate supper, Ryan, Ally, and Dillon went off to the cottages while Frank and Wanda stayed behind to wash dishes and clean up the kitchen.

"You'd think, as I *am* on vacation, that I'd at least be spared the duties of a scullery wench," Wanda said, standing in front of the sink with one arm immersed in sudsy water. She handed a plate to Frank so he could rinse it in the adjacent sink.

"Don't you mean scullery maid?" Frank said, smirking as he dried the plate and placed it on a stack of plates waiting to be put on a shelf.

"You know what I mean." Wanda flicked her right hand out of the soapy water and splashed Frank.

"Me lady, must I report you to the innkeeper?"

"Perhaps you would like—"

"You guys have to come out and see this," Celeste shouted excitedly, dashing into the mess hall.

Frank and Wanda turned and looked over the serving counter.

"Come on! Hurry!" Celeste waved for them to follow her and ran out of the room.

"Sounds urgent," Frank said and handed the dishtowel to Wanda so she could dry her hand and wipe off the soapsuds she had splashed on her sling.

They hurried through the mess hall and turned down the corridor. Frank could hear voices outside. He opened the door that led onto the observation deck where everyone had gathered.

"What's going on?" Frank asked, letting Wanda go out ahead of him.

Ally turned and said, "Something weird down at the lake."

"Yeah, check it out," Ryan said, pointing down the sloping terrain at the large body of water.

Frank and Wanda came over to take a look.

"It's like the water's dancing," Dillon said as he looked up at his mother.

Isoba and his two daughters were also on the deck, witnessing the phenomena.

Dr. Tomie opened the side door of her office to see what the commotion was all about. She leaned against the doorframe while Samson sat beside her in the open doorway.

Frank gazed down at the lake, which took up about five acres. The entire surface seemed to be flittering, not sparkling, as he'd seen it do just before an evening sunset.

This was completely different.

"What do you think it is?" Wanda asked.

But before Frank could answer, a huge swarm rose off the lake, like a giant malevolent cloud—and it was heading straight for the observation deck.

"Oh my God, Frank, there're millions of them," Wanda gasped.

"Everyone, get inside!" Frank yelled.

Dr. Tomie pulled Samson away from the doorway and stepped back to make room as everyone dashed into her office to escape the winged horde.

Isoba was the last one in and closed the door but not before the room was engulfed with mayflies.

Ryan swatted his face while Ally tried to get them out of her hair. Dillon was having fun trying to catch the bugs while Samson attempted to wedge himself under the desk.

Dayo and Adanna were scooping the tiny insects up with stiff sheets of paper and dumping them into a trash bin while Dr. Tomie covered the top with a folder so that the insects wouldn't fly back out. Isoba and Celeste used their hands to scoop them off the walls.

Frank gazed out the office window at the swarm of mayflies, so thick it was impossible to see more than a couple feet.

He snatched a few out of the air that were flying about the room and glanced at the ones in his palm. The mayflies were in the subimago stage. In an hour or so they would moult into adults with productive sex organs. It always seemed like a cruel joke for a creature to forage for two years as a nymph at the bottom of a lake just to sprout wings for a single day so that it could procreate then die.

"So what do we do now?" Wanda asked.

"I guess we have no choice but to wait," Frank said

**

It was close to midnight by the time the swarm dissipated and a large majority of the mayflies returned to the lake.

Frank, Wanda, and Celeste had remained in the office while the others camped in the mess hall until the mayfly inundation had passed.

Frank opened the office door that led out onto the deck. There were thick piles of dead mayflies on the expansive deck, some as deep as two feet, which would have to later be swept away. He figured the female mayflies were back on the water, each one capable of laying 3,000 eggs at one time.

"Be careful you don't slip," Frank said as Celeste followed him out. He stepped warily, feeling the soles of his boots glide over the squishy bugs. He made his way over to a railing and gazed down at the lake glimmering under the sliver of moonlight.

"Boy, they sure made a mess," Celeste said, walking gingerly.

"Smells like a fish market." Wanda worked her way over to where Frank was standing, sliding her boots across the deck like a cross-country skier then grabbing the railing for support.

A green flash streaked across the night sky, then another, until there was a steady barrage of meteorites racing over the distant savanna—so many blips that the cosmic event was creating an aurora borealis effect of swirling colors in the atmosphere.

Frank, Wanda, and Celeste gawked at the heavens, mesmerized by the incredible display of shooting stars.

Suddenly, a fiery globe swooped down and crashed into the middle of the lake.

"That was a little too close for comfort," Frank said, the three of them watching awestruck while the steam rose on the turbulent point of impact.

61

For the next three days everyone stayed relatively busy. Frank estimated that the mayfly swarm had been in the billions. They devoted some time to sweeping the observation deck and raking up the dead insects in large piles, creating pathways leading out of exterior doorways so no one would slip and fall on the greasy mush.

Celeste continued to monitor the ham radio, hoping for a reply to one of her broadcasts.

Isoba and Adanna had been patrolling the grounds in alternating shifts and decided that they could be more effective establishing a watch station on the roof of the clinic where they could set up some shade and maintain a better view of the surrounding savanna. In the event of trouble, they had an air horn that they could sound to alert everyone in the compound.

Ryan had helped his mother conduct a thorough inventory of the food supplies on hand. Based upon the amount of people that were currently holed up on the reserve, Wanda had determined that there were enough rations to last them three months, longer if they were to hunt for game. Growing a garden didn't seem prudent in the withering African heat.

Water would soon be an issue. Even though there was a well with a moderate amount coming up through the pipe, it was taking exceedingly more hand pumping to draw the liquid up out of the ground. The underground aquifer was probably drying up.

Knowing that their resources were limited, Dr. Tomie decided it was best to tend to the ailing animals in the clinic as best they could before releasing them back into the wild. Ally and Dayo assisted in caring for the injured animals. When Dillon wasn't out in the corral bottle-feeding Lucy, he was sitting on the floor in the clinic surrounded by the litter of wild dog pups, letting them take turns nursing on the bottle.

Frank was just walking into the mess hall to talk with Wanda, who was sitting at a table with Ryan when the air horn blasted outside.

Wanda looked up from her paperwork and gazed over at Frank. "Are we being attacked?"

"I don't know," Frank said. He turned and dashed out into the hall. Wanda and Ryan were right behind him. They raced for the glass door leading out the front of the building. Banging through the door, they immediately shielded their eyes from the glaring sun.

Ryan used the palm of his hand as a visor and gazed up. "Look! It's a plane!"

Frank turned and gazed up at the two figures standing at the edge of the roof.

"Your pilot has returned for you," Isoba called, peering through his binoculars at the approaching aircraft then looking down at Frank.

"Should we pack up our stuff?" Wanda asked.

"Just leave it," Frank said, and looked at Wanda. "There're still five vacant seats on that plane. That means Celeste, and I know she'll balk, but I think we should get Gayle to come with us. There's also enough room for Isoba, Adanna, and Dayo."

"Thank you for the offer, Frank" Dr. Tomie said, halfway out the front door. "But I am afraid I will have to decline. I can't leave the reserve."

"I really don't think it's safe to stay here."

The twin-propeller Beechcraft was making its decent, the two tires under the wings touching down first on the dirt airstrip, followed by the nose landing gear.

As the small private plane taxied toward Frank and the others, he couldn't help noticing the rugged condition of parts of the runway, as if a tractor had driven by and dropped a tow-behind plow and scraped up the surface.

The wing flaps went down and the turbo engines gave enough back thrust to slow the plane to a complete stop.

Ally and Dillon came rushing out of the building and both saw the plane. "Oh my God, does this mean we can go home?" Ally yelped.

"Can Lucy come on the plane?" Dillon asked.

"Honey, I don't think..." Wanda started to say but decided an explanation would have to wait.

The passenger door opened near the rear of the plane and the stairs extended down to the ground. Wearing his freshly pressed captain's uniform, the pilot poked his head out and gave everyone a friendly wave. "Hey, folks! You ready to come aboard?"

By this time, Isoba and Adanna had come down from the roof and joined the bustling group. The pilot's sudden arrival had caught everyone unexpectedly. Snap decisions had to be made. Frank had to figure a way to persuade Dr. Tomie and her staff to come with them.

Celeste came running around the side of the building. She was lugging her black case and computer bag. She glanced quickly at the plane and then at the crowd standing idly in the front of the building. "Jesus, what are you guys waiting for?"

Frank waved his hand in the air to get everyone to quiet down.

The pilot had just come down the steps and was walking under the shade of the plane's wing. He ducked his head slightly and grabbed the bill of his hat and slipped it off to wipe his brow. He stepped back into the direct rays of the sun, and while he was putting his hat back on, he tripped on a thin line...

And disappeared in a flash.

If Frank hadn't been looking directly at the pilot at that exact moment, he wouldn't have known what had just happened. The man was strolling along as happy as can be, and then he was gone.

Except for his muffled, underground scream, which only lasted a couple seconds.

"Frank, where the hell is the pilot?" Wanda gasped.

Everyone stared in disbelief.

Frank could see the slightly raised lid in the dirt not too far from where the pilot had been standing. Judging by the narrow opening under the lip, the cover over the trapdoor spider's lair had to be at least ten feet across—which meant there was one hell of a big spider hiding under there, ready to pounce out, grab another prey, and jump back inside its den before the lid even had time to come down. All in the blink of an eye.

Dr. Tomie hobbled over to Frank who was staring at the plane. She leaned on her crutch. "Would you believe you're looking at a seven-million-dollar airplane?"

"Without a pilot," Frank said, "I'd say it's pretty much worthless, Gayle, wouldn't you agree?"

"I'd say that pretty much sums it up."

62

The next day there was a major attack.

It happened around one in the afternoon after everyone had finished with lunch and was taking an extended break, sitting around the mess hall and chitchatting.

Isoba was the only one topside keeping watch. After completing a 360-degree sweep of the surrounding terrain, Isoba had taken a few minutes to sit under the umbrella to escape the blistering sun, confident there was no imminent danger.

That's when the small army burrowed up out of the ground.

Isoba was taking a drink of water when the first giant *marabunta* climbed up the side of the building and crept onto the roof. He immediately dropped his metal cup and grabbed his rifle. The insect racing towards him on six legs was twice his size. It closed in and opened its mandible jaws, ready to bite him in half.

He fired his rifle three times, each bullet drilling a hole into the giant ant's black skull. Green ichor spurted out and the ant collapsed.

Another humongous ant crawled onto the roof, followed by others.

There was no way Isoba could fight them all. Instead, he went over to a small hatch, opened the lid, dropped his rifle through, and jumped down. By the time he hit the floor, the lid above had already closed, preventing the other ants from chasing after him, though he doubted they could have fit through the narrow opening.

"They are on the roof!" he hollered, snatching his rifle and clambering to his feet.

Frank heard the man yell and came running. He'd made a habit of always carrying a gun and had a forty-five caliber pistol holstered on his hip. "What's up there?" he asked once he saw Isoba.

"Marabunta," Isoba answered.

Frank knew Isoba was referring to the dreaded army ant. It was fearsome enough on a minuscule scale, but unimaginable if the creature was 3500 times bigger than its normal self—twice the size of a man.

And there was no telling how many were outside.

Frank ran down the hall and glanced out one of the windows. He could see the giant ants outside, scampering about the building, some even scaling the outside wall.

"Get to the mess hall," Frank shouted.

By the time the two men rushed into the dining area, everyone was already gathering up their weapons, having heard the loud exchanges out in the hall.

"We're going to make our stand in here!" Frank told the others.

"So, what are we fighting today?" Wanda asked, as if there was a guest lineup of creatures featured for each day of the week.

"They're army ants," Frank said.

"My next question was going to be how many, but as you said *army*, maybe I better not ask."

"I have no idea how many are out there."

"Do you think it would help to barricade the door?" Dr. Tomie asked, leaning against the wall with her crutch.

"That's a good idea," Frank said. "Ryan, Isoba, help me drag some tables over to the doorway. Adanna and Dayo, see if you can find something to nail over that window. Ally, you better keep an eye on your brother." Frank pointed to the long counter that separated the kitchen area from the dining tables. "We'll use that for cover."

After dragging over a couple of tables to block the doorway, Isoba unlocked a side door that led into the adjacent gunroom. He grabbed a cloth sack and quickly filled it with boxes of ammunition. He snatched a couple more rifles off the gun rack and hurried back inside the mess hall.

Adanna and Dayo boarded up the window with a sheet of plywood and some screws.

There was a loud crash of breaking glass from the other side of the building. Frank could hear heavy bodies bustling down the hallway.

"Everybody, get ready!"

Frank moved around the partition and stood in the middle of the group with his rifle aimed at the sole entrance into the dining hall. Wanda was to his left, her good arm outstretched with the Beretta cocked; Adanna, and then her father, both armed with double barrel shotguns, were next to her. Ryan was on Frank's right, the young man also with a hunting rifle. Celeste had a revolver. Dr. Tomie leaned across the counter with her gun pointed across the room.

Ally and Dayo stood behind the shooters, their jobs to pass forward freshly loaded guns and reload the empty firearms; Dillon sat on the floor, waiting eagerly to pass up boxes of ammunition; Samson paced growling at the boy's side, the large Anatolian shepherd's hackles up.

The ragtag group of survivors was in for the fight of their lives.

Suddenly, the wall around the doorframe ripped open and a giant ant entered the room, followed by another and another. They scaled the barrier of tables and rushed across the floor.

"Fire!" Frank yelled.

The barrage of gunfire was deafening as the room began to fill with smoke and the bullets and buckshot blew gaping holes in the giant ants' bodies and shot off their limbs, leaving twitching piles of severed legs.

Frank emptied his rifle and passed it back. Ally slapped another rifle into his hand and he resumed firing.

The gargantuan ants continued to scramble through the opening in the wall. Each time one wedged through, it broke off more of the drywall, until there was enough room for two ants to fit through at the same time.

By now there were over twenty of the giant insects coming at them. Even though the carcasses were piling up and the ants had to scale the bodies of their dead comrades, they still kept coming.

Isoba handed his empty shotgun to Dayo, but she was having trouble opening the breech on the gun she was suppose to hand back to him. He reached down and grabbed a handful of cartridges.

"There's no way we can hold them off," Wanda yelled. She looked down at Dillon. "Dilly, go hide in the pantry."

"But Mom..."

"Do it!" Wanda turned and emptied six rounds into a giant ant as it clambered onto the serving counter. The creature fell back, but others pulled it out of the way with their mandibles and kept advancing.

"Everyone, move back!" Frank yelled, even though there was nowhere for them to go. They were trapped and almost out of ammunition.

Frank watched as the black horde continued to scrabble in.

63

Frank was the last to back into the small space just off the kitchen reserved for the open pantry and the walk-in refrigeration unit; neither one the ideal spot for a last defense. The only advantage was that the walkthrough was only wide enough for a single person, so they were able to keep the monstrous ants at bay, killing the ones foolish enough to try and squeeze through.

As everyone was so clustered together, it was near impossible to fire a weapon without either deafening the next person or getting blinded by the gun blast.

Frank aimed his rifle and pulled the trigger on the next bug to show itself.

The hammer came down and clicked on the firing pin.

"I'm out!"

"Me too," Wanda shouted, using her body to shield Ally and Dillon in the pantry.

The others shook their heads and lowered their weapons.

Frank saw a giant ant climbing up the far wall and another's head protruding out of a chewed section of drywall.

He looked over at the walk-in cooler.

"Everyone inside," he yelled and opened the heavy door.

"But we'll freeze in there," Ryan said.

"Better than to die out here," Frank snapped.

The interior of the unit was eight by twelve feet with generous headroom but as there were racks of shelves on two sides, the standing room was limited, especially for ten people and a big dog. The first thing they did was drag out the jumbled remains of the ant Frank had dissected and was keeping in cold storage so as to make more room.

As soon as Frank pulled the door closed, he could hear a heavy thud up above.

Dr. Tomie checked the thermostat and pushed a button. "The best I can do is set it at 40 degrees."

"If it gets too cold we can always push the safety release," Ally said, pointing to the red knob by the locking handle.

"And then what?" Ryan said. "Invite them in?"

"Come on," Wanda sniped. "Enough bickering. We're going to make it out of this. Right, Frank?"

Frank scowled then shrugged his shoulders. "Yeah, but I wish I knew how."

"Hey, guys!" Celeste cried out. "Did you hear that?"

Outside, the cumbersome ants were clambering all over the refrigeration unit, looking for a way in.

"I don't hear anything," Ryan said.

And then Frank heard rapid machinegun fire. He grabbed the handle and pushed the door open a crack. He gazed up but couldn't see any ants.

"Careful, Frank," Wanda warned. "They may be waiting a trap."

Now that the door was open, the gunfire was extremely loud.

Frank slipped out and edged over to the corner of the wall so he could see what was going on.

Two helmeted soldiers in camouflage fatigues and heavy combat gear were firing high-tech assault rifles that looked like they had been conceived in a science fiction movie. Tracer bullets sliced through the ants like laser beams, each shot accurately targeted to follow the previous hit. Most of the ants were dead; those still alive were just twitching on the ground.

"Hey! We're over here!" Frank shouted, trying to be heard over the din of the gunfire.

Another soldier entered the room. He appeared to be the ranking officer because when he held up his hand the other two men ceased firing. He spotted Frank and immediately walked over.

"Are you Frank Travis? Professor Frank Travis?"

"Yes, that's right."

"Lieutenant Riker, Fourth Platoon Infantry," the man said and raised his visor so Frank could see his face. He was in his early twenties and already had a deep battle scar across his right cheek.

"Can't tell you how glad I am to see you fellows." Frank shook the man's gloved hand. He turned as Wanda and the others came over to join him.

"Is Doctor Celeste Starr here?" Riker asked.

"I am," Celeste answered.

"I have orders to take you both back to our bivouac where you'll be transported back to the States."

"Are you serious?" Wanda asked.

"Yes, ma'am, I'm quite serious," Riker said with a stern face.

"Why me?" Frank asked.

"You were recommended as one of the top entomologists in your field by your university."

"So there have been other attacks?" Frank said, gesturing to the giant ants lying dead all around them. Even as he spoke, an ant raised its head and clacked its mandibles. A soldier waltzed up and killed it with a single shot.

"It's happening everywhere. In some of the cities, the swarms are so bad that they're closing down the commercial airports. There have been reports of metropolitan areas being overrun by giant cockroaches. In parts of Australia, giant weta are decimating crops for hundreds of miles."

"What's a weta?" Dillon asked as he wormed his way in front of Frank so he could get a closer look at the soldier's armament.

"It's like a grasshopper," Frank said, patting the boy on the head.

"Tell him about London," a soldier blurted.

"Remember the rats and how they spread the bubonic plague?" Riker said.

"Don't tell me it's gotten to that?" Frank said.

"Well, not exactly. It seems that giant fleas are eating the rats."

"Oh my God," Ally said.

"That's crazy," Ryan piped in.

"I take it the Astronomical Consortium has been asking for me?" Celeste asked Riker.

"Yes, that is correct," Riker said with a slight nod. "Something to do with a tracking station program that you have developed, I believe."

"What about my family?" Frank asked.

"Well," Riker said, pausing for a beat, "I wasn't given orders to..."

"They don't go, I don't go!"

"Sir, you do realize that I have been instructed to take you by force if need be."

"I'd rather you didn't. I'm sorry, but I can't leave them."

"Very well. Your family can accompany you."

"What about Dr. Tomie, Isoba, and his daughters?" Wanda asked.

"We'll be fine," Dr. Tomie said. "Don't worry about us."

"As our bivouac is not far, I'll have six of my men remain behind, just until I can retrieve them."

"I would really appreciate that," Frank said. "Thanks, Lieutenant."

"You have twenty minutes before we leave."

"You heard the man," Frank said with a grin. "Go pack your bags. We're going home."

64

The tandem-rotary Boeing CH-47 Chinook was the size of a city bus and had landed only fifty feet from the unmanned Beechcraft 10. Four soldiers kept a vigilant perimeter watch around the transport helicopter. The craft's armament consisted of a M240 machinegun on the loading ramp and two similar weapons at each shoulder window behind the cockpit.

Lieutenant Riker stood next to the ramp, his M4 carbine draped across his chest.

Frank and Wanda were the first to come out of their cottage with their bags packed and ready to go. They walked by the other two cottages and waited. Ally bounded out with her travel bag and raced over. Ryan ushered Dillon out the door of their cottage and was carrying both their luggage.

The Chinook was firing up its engines.

"Come on before we miss our ride," Frank said, and they scurried down the pathway that led down to the edge of the dirt airstrip.

As they approached, they ducked their heads as the downdraft of the whirling blades kicked up swirling dust all around them.

Frank was passing one of the soldiers when he caught something out of the corner of his eye by the abandoned airplane. He shielded his eyes from the dirt blowing in his face hoping to get a better look.

The trapdoor spider leapt out of its lair.

Before Frank could yell a warning, the giant arachnid grabbed the soldier and yanked him off his feet.

Another soldier turned and aimed his military shotgun but couldn't get a clean shot without hitting the snared man who was unclipping an M84 from his vest while being dragged across the ground toward the raised lid above the spider's den.

As soon as the soldier was pulled inside, the lid started to fall.

The stun grenade went off with a loud bang and a blinding flash of light.

Riker rushed over and got down on his kneepads. He extended his hand and pulled the soldier out of the hole. The man staggered about, shaking his head like there were bees buzzing around inside his helmet.

The lieutenant strafed the spider pit with his machinegun.

Frank waited as Wanda and the kids scurried up the loading ramp.

He glanced in the cargo hold and saw Celeste already strapped in a canvas seat in a long row of about twenty seats on either side of the fuselage.

Frank started up the ramp and looked back. Lieutenant Riker made a motion with his right arm like he was twirling a lasso, signaling his men to get on board.

Dr. Tomie, Isoba, Adanna, and Dayo were standing in front of the clinic and waving goodbye while the six soldiers left behind stood stoic with their weapons. One of the soldiers—a definite dog fancier—knelt and put his arm across Samson's shoulder.

Once everyone was safely on board and in their seats, the transport helicopter began to lift off.

Frank turned to his left. Two gunners faced opposite shoulder windows just outside the cockpit. The port gunner yanked back the slide on his belt-fed weapon. He yelled, "Incoming nine o'clock!" and fired off a loud barrage.

The helicopter pitched, taking some sort of evasive action.

"What's going on?" Wanda yelled, seated directly across from Frank.

But before he could yell back, the other gunner started firing, the cargo hull sounding like an indoor gun range.

Dillon put both hands over his ears.

"Oh my God!" Ally screamed, turning in her seat.

Frank glanced down the length of the cargo bay and saw a giant yellow jacket fly in and land on the ramp. The wasp's wings brushed against the curved bulkhead as it stepped inside. Everyone started unbuckling their seatbelts to move out of its way.

Lieutenant Riker remained calm, stood up, and walked toward the immense creature, a good two feet taller than he was. He aimed his compact machinegun and rattled off a quick burst.

The tight pattern of bullets punched through the wasp's thorax, causing it to slip back on its own gore that spilled onto the deck plates. Riker fired again. The yellow jacket slid out and fell away.

A gunner yelled, "They've had enough!" and the shooting stopped.

Riker hit the control and the rear ramp began to close.

Everyone returned to their seats to gaze out the portals while the helicopter maintained a low altitude over the savanna. Frank spotted Gatura's village but couldn't see anyone outside the dwellings.

"Look, there's Sasha," Ally yelled, her nose to the glass.

Frank caught a glimpse of the white lioness, her young cub, and the rest of the pride, heading for the foothills.

He remembered when they first arrived and flew over the thundering herds of wildebeest and zebras stampeding majestically across the savanna.

Now all he could see was small groups of panic-stricken animals trying to outrun mammoth insects that shouldn't even exist. Thousands of monstrous army ants were crawling out of burrows in the ground like debris spewing out of a backed up drain. An enormous black button spider was clinging onto the back of an elephant that was trying to keep up with the fleeing herd. Frank knew the deadly venom had to be swift when he saw the big gray stumble and fall.

Swarms of immense blowflies and other humongous insects were feeding on the hundreds of animal carcasses littering the prairie.

He sat back in his seat and closed his eyes to clear his head of the nightmare he had just witnessed.

"You okay?" Wanda asked, moving over to sit next to her husband.

Frank opened his eyes and looked at her. "I guess."

Celeste leaned forward in her seat. "So, Frank. Think we can save the world?"

"One can only pray."

65

It had been 157 days since the crew on the International Space Station had any contact with Ground Control or anyone on Earth for that matter; and now Flight Engineer Cass Freeman was the lone survivor on the habitable artificial satellite that was soon to become uninhabitable.

That tranquil feeling she'd once experienced drifting around the planet like a leaf spinning endlessly in a mountain stream had changed drastically to tumbling in a clothes drier filled with rocks.

Every piece of external equipment on the ISS had been damaged or destroyed passing through the asteroid belt, which for some unexplainable reason had attached itself to Earth's orbital ring and refused to leave, much like a blood-bloated tick on a dog.

Before the last science officer had suffocated due to an airlock breach, she'd alluded to a theory that the denser asteroids were acting as a cheese grater, shredding the 3000 manmade satellites as they passed through the belt.

Cass gazed out the observation dome as the sea of space junk floated by; crushed motor housings, shattered solar panels, and mangled antennas.

The tiny living organisms on the other side of the pitted glass looked like something from a bad cold left on a sneeze guard at a salad bar.

The ISS was completing its pass over the dark side of the planet. Areas that had been dense cities were pitch black. She wondered if they would ever restore power.

Another chunk of space rock fell out of orbit and streaked down through the atmosphere. A twisted weather satellite tumbled earthward.

The alien life forms shimmered as an aspheric sliver of sun shone on the glass.

Cass hugged herself and shivered even though she was wearing her long-sleeved jumpsuit and gloves. It was cold as a tomb and soon the life support system would fail.

All her life she had dreamed of being an astronaut and making her family proud. Now she wondered if any of them were even alive. Something terrible was happening down there, and there was nothing she could do about it as she traveled 17,500 miles per hour 250 miles above the planet like a forgotten message in a bottle.

She gazed down at the Northern Hemisphere and the Great Plains. A wispy layer of white cloud cover parted slowly above the flat wheat-colored landscape.

A large mass was moving easterly.

"What the hell is going on down there?" she screamed.

But no one heard her.

Not even the things clinging to the other side of the glass.

66

Twenty-three M1 Abrams of the 41st Armored Calvary Tank Brigade rumbled across the broad expanse of flatland in a single row almost a quarter-mile wide. Each armored vehicle was spaced fifty feet apart from the next, ample room for the lower section of the tank to complete a 360-degree pivot while the turret remained stationary, never once taking its sights off its intended target.

All gun muzzles pointed in the direction of the perspective enemy steadily catching up, giving the appearance that the tanks were retreating in reverse when in reality, it was the turrets that were facing backward.

Engines roared at a cruising speed of 30 miles per hour; steel tracks tore up the lumpy ground and left prairie dog pancakes.

Ryan had only been in for five months and was already Gunners Mate Private First Class and the mechanic on a four-man crew of a sixty-two-ton, four-million-dollar piece of ass-kicking machinery with enough firepower to take down a small army.

Thanks to the shit storm and accelerated boot camp training, worldwide military recruitment was at an all-time high. Fighting for freedom was a thing of the past. The real badge of courage was getting in the trenches defending the human race from extinction.

Standing waist high in the turret's open hatch with the wind buffeting his back, Ryan grabbed both handles on his .50 caliber machinegun and glanced to his right at the other gunners jostling in their tanks, getting their kidneys handed to them as the armored vehicles pounded across the rough open terrain.

He turned, eyes glued on the horizon for the first sign of the enemy. He couldn't help thinking about his family and how everyone had been affected by what was being called an alien invasion.

His stepfather, Frank, said it was more like Mother Nature getting dumped on her head. He had joined a coalition of entomologists and other scientists striving to eliminate the global threat along with Celeste and her associates at the Astronomical Consortium desperately tracking down the meteorite impact sites.

The last time he had heard from his mom, she was heading up the Nor-Cal Militia in a region of California, which had suffered heavy casualties throughout the past few months. He worried about his sister, Ally, a triage volunteer, and missed his little brother, Dillon. They were all living in the Nor-Cal survivor camp. Maybe someday, this would all be over and they could be reunited as a family again.

Rumors were rampant about gargantuan bark beetles devouring the woodlands and the rainforests all over the world, and if they continued at the rate they were going, there wouldn't be a tree left standing in a year's time and the planet's oxygen supply would be depleted.

Bye-bye, Earth.

Ryan was damned if he was going to hand the planet over to a bunch of bugs.

"Hoppers!" a voice boomed in the headset inside his helmet.

He stared out over the grassland and saw a two-mile-wide locust swarm come into view. Even at this distance, he could tell the nomadic grasshoppers were as big as station wagons. It was like a yellow wave rolling over the prairie.

Devouring everything in its path.

The horde took flight and ascended on the tanks.

"Give 'em hell boys!"

Twenty-three .50 caliber machineguns opened fire, obliterating the herbivorous insects. The result looked like yellow graffiti being shot out of a leaf blower. But for each hopper annihilated, there was another to take its place.

Ryan swiveled his weapon and knocked half a dozen out of the air. He heard one of the gunners scream. Some of the tanks were completely engulfed by hoppers.

Two of the Abrams broke ranks, careening into each other.

A giant grasshopper chomped on a gunner's helmet and ripped him out of the hatch.

Every tank unleashed its main and secondary armament: M68 rifled guns, smoothbore cannons, and 10,000-round M240 machineguns.

Ryan watched in horror as one of the tanks covered with hoppers swung the barrel of its cannon and fired at the tank next to it. The armored vehicle exploded. Most of the tanks' drivers were operating blind because the tank commanders couldn't give instructions with the view ports smeared with insect entrails. Gunners were left as the only eyes on the road.

Two F-18 Super Hornets swooped down from the clouds. The lead jet dropped two bombs and laid out a long fiery swath of napalm that ignited hundreds of hoppers into crispy critters.

The second bomber came in for a pass. A massive wall of locust rose in the plane's path. The twin engines sputtered as the turbines choked on the bug guts clogging the vanes. The pilot catapulted out seconds before the aircraft nosed into the ground and went up in a blazing plume of black smoke.

"Rafferty, button it up!" Ryan immediately obeyed his tank commander and dropped down, closing the hatch behind him. He squeezed into the tight quarters and manned the gunner position. He looked at the screen on the thermal viewer, but there were too many images to target.

So they waited until the locust swarm was gone.

They'd lost four tanks that day and sixteen crewmembers, not counting the eight gunners killed—men who died in the defense of their planet.

An hour later, Ryan was back in the open hatch manning his .50 caliber machinegun as the convoy of tanks rolled up to the command base surrounded by a twelve-foot tall solar-powered electrical fence and heavily armed gun towers.

He smiled at the banner he and a few of his buddies had stenciled and hung over the entrance in reference to something his stepfather had once said during a bizarre autopsy: **WELCOME TO THE NEXT WORLD.**

ABOUT THE AUTHOR

Gerry Griffiths lives in San Jose, California, with his family and their five rescue dogs and a cat. He is a Horror Writers Association member, has over thirty published short stories in various anthologies and magazines, as well as a short story collection entitled *Creatures*. He is also the author of *Silurid* and *The Beasts of Stoneclad Mountain*, as well as *Death Crawlers* with the follow-up standalone novels, *Deep in the Jungle* and *The Next World*, all published by Severed Press.

CHECK OUT OTHER GREAT
HORROR NOVELS

BLACK FRIDAY
by Michael Hodges

Jared the kleptomaniac, Chike the unemployed IT guy,
Patricia the shopaholic, and Jeff the meth dealer are
trapped inside a Chicago supermall on Black Friday.
Bridgefield Mall empties during a fire alarm, and most of
the shoppers drive off into a strange mist surrounding the
mall parking lot. They never return. Chike and his group
try calling friends and family, but their smart phones won't
work, not even Twitter. As the mist creeps closer, the mall
lights flicker and surge. Bulbs shatter and spray glass into
the air. Unsettling noises are heard from within the mist, as
the meth dealer becomes unhinged and hunts the group
within the mall. Cornered by the mist, and hunted from
within, Chike and the survivors must fight for their lives
while solving the mystery of what happened to Bridgefield
Mall. Sometimes, a good sale just isn't worth it.

GRIMWEAVE
by Tim Curran

In the deepest, darkest jungles of Indochina, an ancient
evil is waiting in a forgotten, primeval valley. It is patient,
monstrous, and bloodthirsty. Perfectly adapted to its hot,
steaming environment, it strikes silent and stealthy, it
chosen prey: human. Now Michael Spiers, a Marine sniper,
the only survivor of a previous encounter with the beast, is
going after it again. Against his better judgement, he is
made part of a Marine Force Recon team that will hunt it
down and destroy it.

The hunters are about to become the hunted.

CHECK OUT OTHER GREAT HORROR NOVELS

DEATH CRAWLERS
by Gerry Griffiths

Worldwide, there are thought to be 8,000 species of centipede, of which, only 3,000 have been scientifically recorded. The venom of Scolopendra gigantea—the largest of the arthropod genus found in the Amazon rainforest—is so potent that it is fatal to small animals and toxic to humans. But when a cargo plane departs the Amazon region and crashes inside a national park in the United States, much larger and deadlier creatures escape the wreckage to roam wild, reproducing at an astounding rate. Entomologist, Frank Travis solicits small town sheriff Wanda Rafferty's help and together they investigate the crash site. But as a rash of gruesome deaths befalls the townsfolk of Prospect, Frank and Wanda will soon discover how vicious and cunning these new breed of predators can be. Meanwhile, Jake and Nora Carver, and another backpacking couple, are venturing up into the mountainous terrain of the park. If only they knew their fun-filled weekend is about to become a living nightmare.

THE PULLER
by Michael Hodges

Matt Kearns has two choices: fight or hide. The creature in the orchard took the rest. Three days ago, he arrived at his favorite place in the world, a remote shack in Michigan's Upper Peninsula. The plan was to mourn his father's death and figure out his life. Now he's fighting for it. An invisible creature has him trapped. Every time Matt tries to flee, he's dragged backwards by an unseen force. Alone and with no hope of rescue, Matt must escape the Puller's reach. But how do you free yourself from something you cannot see?

CHECK OUT OTHER GREAT HORROR NOVELS

MONSTROSITY
by **Tim Curran**

The Food. It seeped from the ground, a living, gushing, teratogenic nightmare. It contaminated anything that ate it, causing nature to run wild with horrible mutations, creating massive monstrosities that roam the land destroying towns and cities, feeding on livestock and human beings and one another. Now Frank Bowman, an ordinary farmer with no military skills, must get his children to safety. And that will mean a trip through the contaminated zone of monsters, madmen, and The Food itself. Only a fool would attempt it. Or a man with a mission.

THE SQUIRMING
by **Jack Hamlyn**

You are their hosts

You are their food.

The parasites came out of nowhere, squirming horrors that enslaved the human race. They turned the population into mindless pack animals, psychotic cannibalistic hordes whose only purpose was to feed them.

Now with the human race teetering at the edge of extinction, extermination teams are fighting back, killing off the parasites and their voracious hosts. Taking them out one by one in violent, bloody encounters.

The future of mankind is at stake.

And time is running out.

www.ingramcontent.com/pod-product-compliance
Lightning Source LLC
Chambersburg PA
CBHW051949170626
46808CB00007B/2541